William Watson

The Collected Poems of William Watson

William Watson

The Collected Poems of William Watson

ISBN/EAN: 9783337206802

Printed in Europe, USA, Canada, Australia, Japan

Cover: Foto ©Andreas Hilbeck / pixelio.de

More available books at **www.hansebooks.com**

COLLECTED POEMS

WILLIAM·WATSON·
MDCCC·XCVIII·

THE COLLECTED POEMS

OF

WILLIAM WATSON

JOHN LANE

NEW YORK AND LONDON

M DCCC XCIX

THE UNIVERSITY PRESS, CAMBRIDGE, U. S. A.

TO

THE RIGHT HONOURABLE
THE EARL OF ROSEBERY, K.G., K.T.

THESE POEMS

ARE COLLECTIVELY DEDICATED

IN GRATEFUL MEMORY

OF THE GENEROUS APPRECIATION

WITH WHICH HE HAS ALREADY

DISTINGUISHED THEM

PREFATORY

In preparing this Collected Edition of his poems the Author has excluded the whole of his earliest volume, " The Prince's Quest " (1880); has omitted some three-fifths of his second volume, "Epigrams" (1884); and has included the greater part of the contents of all his subsequent volumes of verse, with the exception of the " Year of Shame," here represented by a small selection, and " The Eloping Angels," omitted altogether.

The seven sonnets here given, from a sequence of fifteen published in June 1885 under the title of " Ver Tenebrosum," need not be taken as in each case accurately reflecting his present opinions upon events of that year, but are retained for the sake of such purely literary interest as they may possess for certain of his readers.

In a few other poems, widely separated in date of production, and relating to matters of deeper import than that of political controversy or international affairs, he can lay claim to no obstinate consistency of view; and if some of his readers are disposed to regret that while he has grown older his faith has not become more buoyant, he can only ask them to extend a kindly tolerance to one who, even as they, is sincere in his quest of Truth.

CONTENTS

CONTENTS

CONTENTS

xi

CONTENTS

CONTENTS

CONTENTS

WORDSWORTH'S GRAVE

I

THE old rude church, with bare, bald tower, is here:
  Beneath its shadow high-born Rotha flows:
Rotha, remembering well who slumbers near,
  And with cool murmur lulling his repose.

Rotha, remembering well who slumbers near.
  His hills, his lakes, his streams are with him yet.
Surely the heart that read her own heart clear
  Nature forgets not soon: 'tis we forget.

We that with vagrant soul his fixity
  Have slighted; faithless, done his deep faith wrong
Left him for poorer loves, and bowed the knee
  To misbegotten strange new gods of song.

Yet, led by hollow ghost or beckoning elf
    Far from her homestead to the desert bourn,
The vagrant soul returning to herself
    Wearily wise, must needs to him return.

To him and to the powers that with him dwell :—
    Inflowings that divulged not whence they came :
And that secluded spirit unknowable,
    The mystery we make darker with a name :

The Somewhat which we name but cannot know,
    Ev'n as we name a star and only see
His quenchless flashings forth, which ever show
    And ever hide him, and which are not he.

II

Poet who sleepest by this wandering wave !
    When thou wast born, what birth-gift hadst thou
        then ?
To thee what wealth was that the Immortals gave,
    The wealth thou gavest in thy turn to men ?

WORDSWORTH'S GRAVE

Not Milton's keen, translunar music thine ;
  Not Shakespeare's cloudless, boundless human
      view ;
Not Shelley's flush of rose on peaks divine ;
  Nor yet the wizard twilight Coleridge knew.

What hadst thou that could make so large amends
  For all thou hadst not and thy peers possessed,
Motion and fire, swift means to radiant ends ? —
  Thou hadst, for weary feet, the gift of rest.

From Shelley's dazzling glow or thunderous haze,
  From Byron's tempest-anger, tempest-mirth,
Men turned to thee and found—not blast and
      blaze,
  Tumult of tottering heavens, but peace on earth.

Nor peace that grows by Lethe, scentless flower,
  There in white languors to decline and cease :
But peace whose names are also rapture, power,
  Clear sight, and love : for these are parts of peace.

III

I hear it vouched the Muse is with us still ;—
   If less divinely frenzied than of yore,
In lieu of feelings she has wondrous skill
   To simulate emotion felt no more.

Not such the authentic Presence pure, that made
   This valley vocal in the great days gone !—
In *his* great days, while yet the spring-time played
   About him, and the mighty morning shone.

No word-mosaic artificer, he sang
   A lofty song of lowly weal and dole.
Right from the heart, right to the heart it sprang,
   Or from the soul leapt instant to the soul.

He felt the charm of childhood, grace of youth,
   Grandeur of age, insisting to be sung.
The impassioned argument was simple truth
   Half-wondering at its own melodious tongue.

Impassioned ? ay, to the song's ecstatic core !
  But far removed were clangour, storm and feud ;
For plenteous health was his, exceeding store
  Of joy, and an impassioned quietude.

IV

A hundred years ere he to manhood came,
  Song from celestial heights had wandered down,
Put off her robe of sunlight, dew and flame,
  And donned a modish dress to charm the Town.

Thenceforth she but festooned the porch of things ;
  Apt at life's lore, incurious what life meant.
Dextrous of hand, she struck her lute's few strings ;
  Ignobly perfect, barrenly content.

Unflushed with ardour and unblanched with awe,
  Her lips in profitless derision curled,
She saw with dull emotion—if she saw—
  The vision of the glory of the world.

The human masque she watched, with dreamless
    eyes
  In whose clear shallows lurked no trembling
    shade :
The stars, unkenned by her, might set and rise,
  Unmarked by her, the daisies bloom and fade.

The age grew sated with her sterile wit.
  Herself waxed weary on her loveless throne.
Men felt life's tide, the sweep and surge of it,
  And craved a living voice, a natural tone.

For none the less, though song was but half true,
  The world lay common, one abounding theme.
Man joyed and wept, and fate was ever new,
  And love was sweet, life real, death no dream.

In sad stern verse the rugged scholar-sage
  Bemoaned his toil unvalued, youth uncheered.
His numbers wore the vesture of the age,
  But, 'neath it beating, the great heart was heard.

6

WORDSWORTH'S GRAVE

From dewy pastures, uplands sweet with thyme,
   A virgin breeze freshened the jaded day.
It wafted Collins' lonely vesper-chime,
   It breathed abroad the frugal note of Gray.

It fluttered here and there, nor swept in vain
   The dusty haunts where futile echoes dwell,—
Then, in a cadence soft as summer rain,
   And sad from Auburn voiceless, drooped and fell.

It drooped and fell, and one 'neath northern skies,
   With southern heart, who tilled his father's field,
Found Poesy a-dying, bade her rise
   And touch quick Nature's hem and go forth
      healed.

On life's broad plain the ploughman's conquering
      share
   Upturned the fallow lands of truth anew,
And o'er the formal garden's trim parterre
   The peasant's team a ruthless furrow drew.

7

Bright was his going forth, but clouds ere long
   Whelmed him; in gloom his radiance set, and
      those
Twin morning stars of the new century's song,
   Those morning stars that sang together, rose.

In elvish speech the *Dreamer* told his tale
   Of marvellous oceans swept by fateful wings.—
The *Seër* strayed not from earth's human pale,
   But the mysterious face of common things

He mirrored as the moon in Rydal Mere
   Is mirrored, when the breathless night hangs blue.
Strangely remote she seems and wondrous near,
   And by some nameless difference born anew.

V

Peace—peace—and rest! Ah, how the lyre is loth,
   Or powerless now, to give what all men seek!
Either it deadens with ignoble sloth
   Or deafens with shrill tumult, loudly weak.

WORDSWORTH'S GRAVE

Where is the singer whose large notes and clear
   Can heal and arm and plenish and sustain?
Lo, one with empty music floods the ear,
   And one, the heart refreshing, tires the brain.

And idly tuneful, the loquacious throng
   Flutter and twitter, prodigal of time,
And little masters make a toy of song
   Till grave men weary of the sound of rhyme.

And some go prankt in faded antique dress,
   Abhorring to be hale and glad and free;
And some parade a conscious naturalness,
   The scholar's not the child's simplicity.

Enough;—and wisest who from words forbear.
   The kindly river rails not as it glides;
And suave and charitable, the winning air
   Chides not at all, or only him who chides.

VI

Nature! we storm thine ear with choric notes.
   Thou answerest through the calm great nights
      and days,
" Laud me who will : not tuneless are your throats ;
   Yet if ye paused I should not miss the praise."

We falter, half-rebuked, and sing again.
   We chant thy desertness and haggard gloom,
Or with thy splendid wrath inflate the strain,
   Or touch it with thy colour and perfume.

One, his melodious blood aflame for thee,
   Wooed with fierce lust, his hot heart world-defiled.
One, with the upward eye of infancy,
   Looked in thy face, and felt himself thy child.

Thee he approached without distrust or dread—
   Beheld thee throned, an awful queen, above--
Climbed to thy lap and merely laid his head
   Against thy warm wild heart of mother-love.

WORDSWORTH'S GRAVE

He heard that vast heart beating—thou didst press
    Thy child so close, and lov'dst him unaware.
Thy beauty gladdened him; yet he scarce less
    Had loved thee, had he never found thee fair!

For thou wast not as legendary lands
    To which with curious eyes and ears we roam.
Nor wast thou as a fane 'mid solemn sands,
    Where palmers halt at evening. Thou wast
        home.

And here, at home, still bides he; but he sleeps;
    Not to be wakened even at thy word:
Though we, vague dreamers, dream he somewhere
        keeps
    An ear still open to thy voice still heard, -

Thy voice, as heretofore, about him blown,
    For ever blown about his silence now;
Thy voice, though deeper, yet so like his own
    That almost, when he sang, we deemed 'twas
        thou!

VII

Behind Helm Crag and Silver Howe the sheen
    Of the retreating day is less and less.
Soon will the lordlier summits, here unseen,
    Gather the night about their nakedness.

The half-heard bleat of sheep comes from the hill.
    Faint sounds of childish play are in the air.
The river murmurs past.   All else is still.
    The very graves seem stiller than they were.

Afar though nation be on nation hurled,
    And life with toil and ancient pain depressed,
Here one may scarce believe the whole wide world
    Is not at peace, and all man's heart at rest.

Rest! 'twas the gift *he* gave; and peace! the shade
    He spread, for spirits fevered with the sun.
To him his bounties are come back—here laid
    In rest, in peace, his labour nobly done.

1884–87.

SHELLEY'S CENTENARY

(4TH AUGUST 1892)

WITHIN a narrow span of time,
Three princes of the realm of rhyme,
At height of youth or manhood's prime
    From earth took wing,
To join the fellowship sublime
    Who, dead, yet sing.

He, first, his earliest wreath who wove
Of laurel grown in Latmian grove,
Conquered by pain and hapless love
    Found calmer home,
Roofed by the heaven that glows above
    Eternal Rome.

SHELLEY'S CENTENARY

A fiercer soul, its own fierce prey,
And cumbered with more mortal clay,
At Missolonghi flamed away,
 And left the air
Reverberating to this day
 Its loud despair.

Alike remote from Byron's scorn
And Keats's magic as of morn
Bursting for ever newly-born
 On forests old,
To wake a hoary world forlorn
 With touch of gold,

Shelley, the cloud-begot, who grew
Nourished on air and sun and dew,
Into that Essence whence he drew
 His life and lyre
Was fittingly resolved anew
 Through wave and fire.

SHELLEY'S CENTENARY

'Twas like his rapid soul!   'Twas meet
That he, who brooked not Time's slow feet,
With passage thus abrupt and fleet
  Should hurry hence,
Eager the Great Perhaps to greet
  With Why? and Whence?

Impatient of the world's fixed way,
He ne'er could suffer God's delay,
But all the future in a day
  Would build divine,
And the whole past in ruins lay,
  An emptied shrine.

Vain vision! but the glow, the fire,
The passion of benign desire,
The glorious yearning, lift him higher
  Than many a soul
That mounts a million paces nigher
  Its meaner goal.

And power is his, if naught besides,
In that thin ether where he rides,
Above the roar of human tides
    To ascend afar,
Lost in a storm of light that hides
    His dizzy car.

Below, the unhasting world toils on,
And here and there are victories won,
Some dragon slain, some justice done,
    While, through the skies,
A meteor rushing on the sun,
    He flares and dies.

But, as he cleaves yon ether clear,
Notes from the unattempted Sphere
He scatters to the enchanted ear
    Of earth's dim throng,
Whose dissonance doth more endear
    The showering song.

In other shapes than he forecast
The world is moulded : his fierce blast,—
His wild assault upon the Past,—
    These things are vain ;
Revolt is transient : what *must* last
    Is that pure strain,

Which seems the wandering voices blent
Of every virgin element, —
A sound from ocean caverns sent,—
    An airy call
From the pavilioned firmament
    O'erdoming all.

And in this world of worldlings, where
Souls rust in apathy, and ne'er
A great emotion shakes the air,
    And life flags tame,
And rare is noble impulse, rare
    The impassioned aim,

SHELLEY'S CENTENARY

'Tis no mean fortune to have heard
A singer who, if errors blurred
His sight, had yet a spirit stirred
  By vast desire,
And ardour fledging the swift word
  With plumes of fire.

A creature of impetuous breath.
Our torpor deadlier than death
He knew not; whatsoe'er he saith
  Flashes with life :
He spurreth men, he quickeneth
  To splendid strife.

And in his gusts of song he brings
Wild odours shaken from strange wings,
And unfamiliar whisperings
  From far lips blown,
While all the rapturous heart of things
  Throbs through his own,—

His own that from the burning pyre

One who had loved his wind-swept lyre

Out of the sharp teeth of the fire

    Unmolten drew,

Beside the sea that in her ire

    Smote him and slew.

LACHRYMÆ MUSARUM

(6th October 1892)

LOW, like another's, lies the laurelled head:
The life that seemed a perfect song is o'er:
Carry the last great bard to his last bed.
Land that he loved, thy noblest voice is mute.
Land that he loved, that loved him! nevermore
Meadow of thine, smooth lawn or wild sea-shore,
Gardens of odorous bloom and tremulous fruit,
Or woodlands old, like Druid couches spread,
The master's feet shall tread.
Death's little rift hath rent the faultless lute:
The singer of undying songs is dead.

Lo, in this season pensive-hued and grave,
While fades and falls the doomed, reluctant leaf
20

LACHRYMÆ MUSARUM

From withered Earth's fantastic coronal,
With wandering sighs of forest and of wave
Mingles the murmur of a people's grief
For him whose leaf shall fade not, neither fall.
He hath fared forth, beyond these suns and
    showers.
For us, the autumn glow, the autumn flame,
And soon the winter silence shall be ours:
Him the eternal spring of fadeless fame
Crowns with no mortal flowers.

What needs his laurel our ephemeral tears,
To save from visitation of decay?
Not in this temporal light alone, that bay
Blooms, nor to perishable mundane ears
Sings he with lips of transitory clay.
Rapt though he be from us,
Virgil salutes him, and Theocritus;
Catullus, mightiest-brained Lucretius, each
Greets him, their brother, on the Stygian beach;
Proudly a gaunt right hand doth Dante reach;
Milton and Wordsworth bid him welcome home:

LACHRYMÆ MUSARUM

Keats, on his lips the eternal rose of youth,

Doth in the name of Beauty that is Truth

A kinsman's love beseech ;

Coleridge, his locks aspersed with fairy foam,

Calm Spenser, Chaucer suave,

His equal friendship crave :

And godlike spirits hail him guest, in speech

Of Athens, Florence, Weimar, Stratford, Rome.

He hath returned to regions whence he came.

Him doth the spirit divine

Of universal loveliness reclaim.

All nature is his shrine.

Seek him henceforward in the wind and sea,

In earth's and air's emotion or repose,

In every star's august serenity,

And in the rapture of the flaming rose.

There seek him if ye would not seek in vain,

There, in the rhythm and music of the Whole :

Yea, and for ever in the human soul

Made stronger and more beauteous by his strain.

LACHRYMÆ MUSARUM

For lo ! creation's self is one great choir,
And what is nature's order but the rhyme
Whereto in holiest unanimity
All things with all things move unfalteringly,
Infolded and communal from their prime ?
Who shall expound the mystery of the lyre ?
In far retreats of elemental mind
Obscurely comes and goes
The imperative breath of song, that as the
    wind
Is trackless, and oblivious whence it blows.
Demand of lilies wherefore they are white,
Extort her crimson secret from the rose,
But ask not of the Muse that she disclose
The meaning of the riddle of her might :
Somewhat of all things sealed and recondite,
Save the enigma of herself, she knows.
The master could not tell, with all his lore,
Wherefore he sang, or whence the mandate
    sped :
Ev'n as the linnet sings, so I, he said ;—
Ah, rather as the imperial nightingale,

LACHRYMÆ MUSARUM

That held in trance the ancient Attic shore,
And charms the ages with the notes that o'er
All woodland chants immortally prevail!
And now, from our vain plaudits greatly fled,
He with diviner silence dwells instead,
And on no earthly sea with transient roar,
Unto no earthly airs, he trims his sail,
But far beyond our vision and our hail
Is heard for ever and is seen no more.

No more, O never now,
Lord of the lofty and the tranquil brow
Whereon nor snows of time
Have fall'n, nor wintry rime,
Shall men behold thee, sage and mage sublime.
Once, in his youth obscure,
The maker of this verse, which shall endure
By splendour of its theme that cannot die,
Beheld thee eye to eye,
And touched through thee the hand
Of every hero of thy race divine,
Ev'n to the sire of all the laurelled line,

LACHRYMÆ MUSARUM

The sightless wanderer on the Ionian strand,
With soul as healthful as the poignant brine,
Wide as his skies and radiant as his seas,
Starry from haunts of his Familiars nine,
Glorious Mæonides.
Yea, I beheld thee, and behold thee yet:
Thou hast forgotten, but can I forget?
The accents of thy pure and sovereign tongue.
Are they not ever goldenly impressed
On memory's palimpsest?
I see the wizard locks like night that hung,
I tread the floor thy hallowing feet have trod:
I see the hands a nation's lyre that strung,
The eyes that looked through life and gazed on
      God.

   The seasons change, the winds they shift and
      veer;
The grass of yesteryear
Is dead; the birds depart, the groves decay:
Empires dissolve and peoples disappear:
Song passes not away.

LACHRYMÆ MUSARUM

Captains and conquerors leave a little dust,
And kings a dubious legend of their reign;
The swords of Cæsars, they are less than rust:
The poet doth remain.
Dead is Augustus, Maro is alive;
And thou, the Mantuan of our age and clime,
Like Virgil shalt thy race and tongue survive,
Bequeathing no less honeyed words to time,
Embalmed in amber of eternal rhyme,
And rich with sweets from every Muse's hive;
While to the measure of the cosmic rune
For purer ears thou shalt thy lyre attune,
And heed no more the hum of idle praise
In that great calm our tumults cannot reach,
Master who crown'st our immelodious days
With flower of perfect speech.

TO EDWARD DOWDEN

ON RECEIVING FROM HIM A COPY OF "THE LIFE
OF SHELLEY"

FIRST, ere I slake my hunger, let me thank
The giver of the feast.   For feast it is,
Though of ethereal, translunary fare—
His story who pre-eminently of men
Seemed nourished upon starbeams and the stuff
Of rainbows, and the tempest, and the foam :
Who hardly brooked on his impatient soul
The fleshly trammels ; whom at last the sea
Gave to the fire, from whose wild arms the winds
Took him, and shook him broadcast to the world.

In my young days of fervid poesy
He drew me to him with his strange far light,—
He held me in a world all clouds and gleams,

TO EDWARD DOWDEN

And vasty phantoms, where ev'n Man himself
Moved like a phantom 'mid the clouds and gleams.
Anon the Earth recalled me, and a voice
Murmuring of dethroned divinities
And dead times deathless upon sculptured urn—
And Philomela's long-descended pain
Flooding the night—and maidens of romance
To whom asleep St. Agnes' love-dreams come
Awhile constrained me to a sweet duresse
And thraldom, lapping me in high content,
Soft as the bondage of white amorous arms.
And then a third voice, long unheeded - held
Claustral and cold, and dissonant and tame—
Found me at last with ears to hear.   It sang
Of lowly sorrows and familiar joys,
Of simple manhood, artless womanhood,
And childhood fragrant as the limpid morn;
And from the homely matter nigh at hand
Ascending and dilating, it disclosed
Spaces and avenues, calm heights and breadths
Of vision, whence I saw each blade of grass
With roots that groped about eternity.

TO EDWARD DOWDEN

And in each drop of dew upon each blade
The mirror of the inseparable All.
The first voice, then the second, in their turns
Had sung me captive.   This voice sang me free.
Therefore, above all vocal sons of men,
Since him whose sightless eyes saw hell and heaven,
To Wordsworth be my homage, thanks, and love.
Yet dear is Keats, a lucid presence, great
With somewhat of a glorious soullessness.
And dear, and great with an excess of soul,
Shelley, the hectic flamelike rose of verse,
All colour, and all odour, and all bloom,
Steeped in the noonlight, glutted with the sun,
But somewhat lacking root in homely earth,
Lacking such human moisture as bedews
His not less starward stem of song, who, rapt
Not less in glowing vision, yet retained
His clasp of the prehensible, retained
The warm touch of the world that lies to hand,
Not in vague dreams of man forgetting men,
Nor in vast morrows losing the to-day ;
Who trusted nature, trusted fate, nor found

TO EDWARD DOWDEN

An Ogre, sovereign on the throne of things ;
Who felt the incumbence of the unknown, yet bore
Without resentment the Divine reserve ;
Who suffered not his spirit to dash itself
Against the crags and wavelike break in spray,
But 'midst the infinite tranquillities
Moved tranquil, and henceforth, by Rotha stream
And Rydal's mountain-mirror, and where flows
Yarrow thrice sung or Duddon to the sea,
And wheresoe'er man's heart is thrilled by tones
Struck from man's lyric heartstrings, shall survive.

EPIGRAM

'TIS human fortune's happiest height, to be
  A spirit melodious, lucid, poised, and whole;
Second in order of felicity
  I hold it, to have walk'd with such a soul.

AUTUMN

THOU burden of all songs the earth hath sung,
  Thou retrospect in Time's reverted eyes,
  Thou metaphor of everything that dies,
That dies ill-starred, or dies beloved and young
      And therefore blest and wise,—
O be less beautiful, or be less brief,
  Thou tragic splendour, strange, and full of fear!
  In vain her pageant shall the Summer rear?
At thy mute signal, leaf by golden leaf,
      Crumbles the gorgeous year.

Ah, ghostly as remembered mirth, the tale
  Of Summer's bloom, the legend of the Spring!
  And thou, too, flutterest an impatient wing,
Thou presence yet more fugitive and frail,
      Thou most unbodied thing.

32

AUTUMN

Whose very being is thy going hence,
    And passage and departure all thy theme;
    Whose life doth still a splendid dying seem,
And thou at height of thy magnificence
        A figment and a dream.

Stilled is the virgin rapture that was June,
    And cold is August's panting heart of fire;
    And in the storm-dismantled forest-choir
For thine own elegy thy winds attune
        Their wild and wizard lyre:
And poignant grows the charm of thy decay,
    The pathos of thy beauty, and the sting,
    Thou parable of greatness vanishing!
For me, thy woods of gold and skies of grey
        With speech fantastic ring.

For me, to dreams resigned, there come and go,
    'Twixt mountains draped and hooded night and
        morn,
    Elusive notes in wandering wafture borne,

AUTUMN

From undiscoverable lips that blow
    An immaterial horn;
And spectral seem thy winter-boding trees,
   Thy ruinous bowers and drifted foliage wet—
   O Past and Future in sad bridal met,
O voice of everything that perishes,
    And soul of all regret!

WORLD-STRANGENESS

STRANGE the world about me lies,
  Never yet familiar grown—
Still disturbs me with surprise,
  Haunts me like a face half known.

In this house with starry dome,
  Floored with gemlike plains and seas,
Shall I never feel at home,
  Never wholly be at ease?

On from room to room I stray,
  Yet my Host can ne'er espy,
And I know not to this day
  Whether guest or captive I.

35

WORLD-STRANGENESS

So, between the starry dome
   And the floor of plains and seas,
I have never felt at home,
   Never wholly been at ease.

EPIGRAM

THE statue—Buonarotti said—doth wait,
Thrall'd in the block, for me to emancipate.
The poem —saith the poet—wanders free
Till I betray it to captivity.

THE MOCK SELF

FEW friends are mine, though many wights there
    be
Who, meeting oft a phantasm that makes claim
To be myself, and hath my face and name,
And whose thin fraud I wink at privily,
Account this light impostor very me.
What boots it undeceive them, and proclaim
Myself myself, and whelm this cheat with shame?
I care not, so he leave my true self free,
Impose not on me also; but alas!
I too, at fault, bewildered, sometimes take
Him for myself, and far from mine own sight,
Torpid, indifferent, doth mine own self pass;
And yet anon leaps suddenly awake,
And spurns the gibbering mime into the night.

ENGLAND AND HER COLONIES

SHE stands, a thousand-wintered tree,
　By countless morns impearled;
Her broad roots coil beneath the sea,
　Her branches sweep the world;
Her seeds, by careless winds conveyed,
　Clothe the remotest strand
With forests from her scatterings made,
New nations fostered in her shade,
　And linking land with land.

O ye by wandering tempest sown
　'Neath every alien star,
Forget not whence the breath was blown
　That wafted you afar!

39

For ye are still her ancient seed
    On younger soil let fall—
Children of Britain's island-breed,
To whom the Mother in her need
    Perchance may one day call.

TO A POET

TIME, the extortioner, from richest beauty
Takes heavy toll and wrings rapacious duty.
Austere of feature if thou carve thy rhyme,
Perchance 'twill pay the lesser tax to Time.

WHEN birds were songless on the bough
    I heard thee sing.
The world was full of winter, thou
    Wert full of spring.

To-day the world's heart feels anew
    The vernal thrill,
And thine beneath the rueful yew
    Is wintry chill.

FELICITY

A SQUALID, hideous town, where streams run
    black
With vomit of a hundred roaring mills,—
Hither occasion calls me ; and ev'n here,
All in the sable reek that wantonly
Defames the sunlight and deflowers the morn,
One may at least surmise the sky still blue.
Ev'n here, the myriad slaves of the machine
Deem life a boon; and here, in days far sped,
I overheard a kind-eyed girl relate
To her companions, how a favouring chance
By some few shillings weekly had increased
The earnings of her household, and she said :
" So now we are happy, having all we wished,"—
Felicity indeed ! though more it lay
In wanting little than in winning all.

FELICITY

Felicity indeed!   Across the years
To me her tones come back, rebuking; me,
Spreader of toils to snare the wandering Joy
No guile may capture and no force surprise—
Only by them that never wooed her, won.

O curst with wide desires and spacious dreams,
Too cunningly do ye accumulate
Appliances and means of happiness,
E'er to be happy!   Lavish hosts, ye make
Elaborate preparation to receive
A shy and simple guest, who, warned of all
The ceremony and circumstance wherewith
Ye mean to entertain her, will not come.

IN LALEHAM CHURCHYARD *

(18th August 1890)

'TWAS at this season, year by year,
The singer who lies songless here
Was wont to woo a less austere,
    Less deep repose,
Where Rotha to Winandermere
    Unresting flows,—

Flows through a land where torrents call
To far-off torrents as they fall,
And mountains in their cloudy pall
    Keep ghostly state,
And Nature makes majestical
    Man's lowliest fate.

* The burial-place of Matthew Arnold.

45

IN LALEHAM CHURCHYARD

There, 'mid the August glow, still came
He of the twice-illustrious name,
The loud impertinence of fame
    Not loth to flee—
Not loth with brooks and fells to claim
    Fraternity.

Linked with his happy youthful lot,
Is Loughrigg, then, at last forgot?
Nor silent peak nor dalesman's cot
    Looks on his grave.
Lulled by the Thames he sleeps, and not
    By Rotha's wave.

'Tis fittest thus! for though with skill
He sang of beck and tarn and ghyll,
The deep, authentic mountain-thrill
    Ne'er shook his page!
Somewhat of worldling mingled still
    With bard and sage.

IN LALEHAM CHURCHYARD

And 'twere less meet for him to lie
Guarded by summits lone and high
That traffic with the eternal sky
    And hear, unawed,
The everlasting fingers ply
    The loom of God,

Than, in this hamlet of the plain,
A less sublime repose to gain,
Where Nature, genial and urbane,
    To man defers,
Yielding to us the right to reign,
    Which yet is hers.

And nigh to where his bones abide,
The Thames with its unruffled tide
Seems like his genius typified,—
    Its strength, its grace,
Its lucid gleam, its sober pride,
    Its tranquil pace.

But ah ! not his the eventual fate
Which doth the journeying wave await—
Doomed to resign its limpid state
  And quickly grow
Turbid as passion, dark as hate,
  And wide as woe.

Rather, it may be, over-much
He shunned the common stain and smutch,
From soilure of ignoble touch
  Too grandly free,
Too loftily secure in such'
  Cold purity.

But he preserved from chance control
The fortress of his 'stablisht soul ;
In all things sought to see the Whole ;
  Brooked no disguise ;
And set his heart upon the goal,
  Not on the prize.

48

IN LALEHAM CHURCHYARD

With those Elect he shall survive
Who seem not to compete or strive,
Yet with the foremost still arrive,
    Prevailing still :
Spirits with whom the stars connive
    To work their will.

And ye, the baffled many, who,
Dejected, from afar off view
The easily victorious few
    Of calm renown, —
Have ye not your sad glory too,
    And mournful crown ?

Great is the facile conqueror ;
Yet haply he, who, wounded sore,
Breathless, unhorsed, all covered o'er
    With blood and sweat,
Sinks foiled, but fighting evermore,
    Is greater yet.

LIFE WITHOUT HEALTH

BEHOLD life builded as a goodly house
And grown a mansion ruinous
With winter blowing through its crumbling walls!
The master paceth up and down his halls,
And in the empty hours
Can hear the tottering of his towers
And tremor of their bases underground.
And oft he starts and looks around
At creaking of a distant door
Or echo of his footfall on the floor,
Thinking it may be one whom he awaits
And hath for many days awaited,
Coming to lead him through the mouldering
   gates
Out somewhere, from his home dilapidated.

THE FLIGHT OF YOUTH

YOUTH! ere thou be flown away,
Surely one last boon to-day
    Thou'lt bestow—
One last light of rapture give,
Rich and lordly fugitive!
    Ere thou go.

What, thou canst not?　What, all spent?
All thy spells of ravishment
    Pow'rless now?
Gone thy magic out of date?
Gone, all gone that made thee great?—
    Follow thou!

EPIGRAM

THE Poet gathers fruit from every tree,
Yea, grapes from thorns and figs from thistles he.
Pluck'd by his hand, the basest weed that grows
Towers to a lily, reddens to a rose.

UNDER the dark and piny steep
    We watched the storm crash by :
We saw the bright brand leap and leap
    Out of the shattered sky.

The elements were minist'ring
    To make one mortal blest ;
For, peal by peal, you did but cling
    The closer to his breast.

NAY, bid me not my cares to leave,
  Who cannot from their shadow flee.
I do but win a short reprieve,
  'Scaping to pleasure and to thee.

I may, at best, a moment's grace,
  And grant of liberty, obtain ;
Respited for a little space,
  To go back into bonds again.

A PRELUDE

THE mighty poets from their flowing store
Dispense like casual alms the careless ore;
Through throngs of men their lonely way they go,
Let fall their costly thoughts, nor seem to know.—
Not mine the rich and showering hand, that strews
The facile largess of a stintless Muse.
A fitful presence, seldom tarrying long,
Capriciously she touches me to song—
Then leaves me to lament her flight in vain,
And wonder will she ever come again.

ON LANDOR'S "HELLENICS"

COME hither, who grow cloyed to surfeiting
With lyric draughts o'ersweet, from rills that rise
On Hybla not Parnassus mountain : come
With beakers rinsed of the dulcifluous wave
Hither, and see a magic miracle
Of happiest science, the bland Attic skies
True-mirrored by an English well ;—no stream
Whose heaven-belying surface makes the stars
Reel, with its restless idiosyncrasy ;
But well unstirred, save when at times it takes
Tribute of lovers' eyelids, and at times
Bubbles with laughter of some sprite below.

ENGLAND MY MOTHER

I

ENGLAND my mother,
Wardress of waters,
Builder of peoples,
  Maker of men,—

Hast thou yet leisure
Left for the muses?
Heed'st thou the songsmith
  Forging the rhyme?

Deafened with tumults,
How canst thou hearken?
Strident is faction,
  Demos is loud.

57

Lazarus, hungry,
Menaces Dives;
Labour the giant
　　Chafes in his hold.

Yet do the songsmiths
Quit not their forges;
Still on life's anvil
　　Forge they the rhyme.

Still the rapt faces
Glow from the furnace:
Breath of the smithy
　　Scorches their brows.

Yea, and thou hear'st them?
So shall the hammers
Fashion not vainly
　　Verses of gold.

II

Lo, with the ancient
Roots of man's nature
Twines the eternal
   Passion of song.

Ever Love fans it,
Ever Life feeds it :
Time cannot age it,
   Death cannot slay.

Deep in the world-heart
Stand its foundations,
Tangled with all things,
   Twin-made with all.

Nay, what is Nature's
Self, but an endless
Strife toward music,
   Euphony, rhyme ?

ENGLAND MY MOTHER

Trees in their blooming,
Tides in their flowing,
Stars in their circling,
 Tremble with song.

God on His throne is
Eldest of poets:
Unto His measures
 Moveth the Whole.

III

Therefore deride not
Speech of the muses,
England my mother,
 Maker of men.

Nations are mortal,
Fragile is greatness;
Fortune may fly thee,
 Song shall not fly.

Song the all-girdling,
Song cannot perish:
Men shall make music,
   Man shall give ear.

Not while the choric
Chant of creation
Floweth from all things,
   Poured without pause,

Cease we to echo
Faintly the descant
Whereto for ever
   Dances the world.

IV

So let the songsmith
Proffer his rhyme-gift,
England my mother,
   Maker of men.

ENGLAND MY MOTHER

Grey grows thy count'nance,
Full of the ages;
Time on thy forehead
   Sits like a dream:

Song is the potion
All things renewing,
Youth's one elixir,
   Fountain of morn.

Thou, at the world-loom
Weaving thy future,
Fitly may'st temper
   Toil with delight.

Deemest thou, labour
Only is earnest?
Grave is all beauty,
   Solemn is joy.

ENGLAND MY MOTHER

Song is no bauble—
Slight not the songsmith,
England my mother,
    Maker of men.

SCENTLESS flow'rs I bring thee—yet
In thy bosom be they set;
In thy bosom each one grows
Fragrant beyond any rose.

Sweet enough were she who could,
In thy heart's sweet neighbourhood,
Some redundant sweetness thus
Borrow from that overplus.

SHELLEY AND HARRIET

A STAR look'd down from heaven and loved a
    flower
Grown in earth's garden—loved it for an hour.
Let eyes that trace his orbit in the spheres
Refuse not, to a ruin'd rosebud, tears.

AND these—are these indeed the end,
  This grinning skull, this heavy loam?
Do all green ways whereby we wend
  Lead but to yon ignoble home?

Ah well! thine eyes invite to bliss:
  Thy lips are hives of summer still.
I ask not other worlds while this
  Proffers me all the sweets I will.

THE RAVEN'S SHADOW

SEABIRD, elemental sprite,
  Moulded of the sun and spray —
Raven, dreary flake of night
  Drifting in the eye of day—
What in common have ye two,
Meeting 'twixt the blue and blue?

Thou to eastward carriest
  The keen savour of the foam,
Thou dost bear unto the west
  Fragrance from thy woody home,
Where perchance a house is thine
Odorous of the oozy pine.

THE RAVEN'S SHADOW

Eastward thee thy proper cares,
  Things of mighty moment, call;
Thee to westward thine affairs
  Summon, weighty matters all:
I, where land and sea contest,
Watch you eastward, watch you west,

Till, in snares of fancy caught,
  Mystically changed ye seem,
And the bird becomes a thought,
  And the thought becomes a dream,
And the dream, outspread on high,
Lords it o'er the abject sky.

Surely I have known before
  Phantoms of the shapes ye be—
Haunters of another shore
  'Leaguered by another sea.
There my wanderings night and morn
Reconcile me to the bourn.

THE RAVEN'S SHADOW

There the bird of happy wings
    Wafts the ocean-news I crave :
Rumours of an isle he brings
    Gemlike on the golden wave :
But the baleful beak and plume
Scatter immelodious gloom.

Though the flow'rs be faultless made,
    Perfectly to live and die—
Though the bright clouds bloom and fade
    Flow'rlike 'midst a meadowy sky—
Where this raven roams forlorn
Veins of midnight flaw the morn.

He not less will croak and croak
    As he ever caws and caws,
Till the starry dance be broke,
    Till the sphery pæan pause,
And the universal chime
Falter out of tune and time.

THE RAVEN'S SHADOW

Coils the labyrinthine sea
   Duteous to the lunar will,
But some discord stealthily
   Vexes the world-ditty still,
And the bird that caws and caws
Clasps creation with his claws.

HE holds a dubious balance : —yet *that* scale,
Whose freight the world is, surely shall prevail?
No; Cleopatra droppeth into *this*
One counterpoising orient sultry kiss.

THE GLIMPSE

JUST for a day you crossed my life's dull track,
  Put my ignobler dreams to sudden shame,
Went your bright way, and left me to fall back
  On my own world of poorer deed and aim ;

To fall back on my meaner world, and feel
  Like one who, dwelling 'mid some smoke-
    dimmed town,—
In a brief pause of labour's sullen wheel,—
  'Scaped from the street's dead dust and factory's
    frown,—

In stainless daylight saw the pure seas roll,
  Saw mountains pillaring the perfect sky :
Then journeyed home, to carry in his soul
  The torment of the difference till he die.

TO A SEABIRD

FAIN would I have thee barter fates with me,—
Lone loiterer where the shells like jewels be,
Hung on the fringe and frayed hem of the sea.
But no,—'twere cruel, wild-wing'd Bliss! to thee.

WELL he slumbers, greatly slain,
   Who in splendid battle dies;
Deep his sleep in midmost main
   Pillowed upon pearl who lies.

Ease, of all good gifts the best,
   War and wave at last decree:
Love alone denies us rest,
   Crueller than sword or sea.

LUX PERDITA

THINE were the weak, slight hands
That might have taken this strong soul, and bent
Its stubborn substance to thy soft intent,
And bound it unresisting, with such bands
As not the arm of envious heaven had rent.

Thine were the calming eyes
That round my pinnace could have stilled the sea,
And drawn thy voyager home, and bid him be
Pure with their pureness, with their wisdom wise,
Merged in their light, and greatly lost in thee.

But thou—thou passed'st on,
With whiteness clothed of dedicated days,
Cold, like a star; and me in alien ways
Thou leftest following life's chance lure, where shone
The wandering gleam that beckons and betrays.

"THE THINGS THAT ARE MORE EXCELLENT"

As we wax older on this earth,
    Till many a toy that charmed us seems
Emptied of beauty, stripped of worth,
    And mean as dust and dead as dreams,—
For gauds that perished, shows that passed,
    Some recompense the Fates have sent :
Thrice lovelier shine the things that last,
    The things that are more excellent.

Tired of the Senate's barren brawl,
    An hour with silence we prefer,
Where statelier rise the woods than all
    Yon towers of talk at Westminster.

76

"THINGS THAT ARE MORE EXCELLENT"

Let this man prate and that man plot,
　　On fame or place or title bent :
The votes of veering crowds are not
　　The things that are more excellent.

Shall we perturb and vex our soul
　　For "wrongs" which no true freedom mar,
Which no man's upright walk control,
　　And from no guiltless deed debar?
What odds though tonguesters heal, or leave
　　Unhealed, the grievance they invent?
To things, not phantoms, let us cleave—
　　The things that are more excellent.

Nought nobler is, than to be free :
　　The stars of heaven are free because
In amplitude of liberty
　　Their joy is to obey the laws.
From servitude to freedom's *name*
　　Free thou thy mind in bondage pent :
Depose the fetich, and proclaim
　　The things that are more excellent.

"THINGS THAT ARE MORE EXCELLENT"

And in appropriate dust be hurled
    That dull, punctilious god, whom they
That call their tiny clan the world,
    Serve and obsequiously obey :
Who con their ritual of Routine,
    With minds to one dead likeness blent,
And never ev'n in dreams have seen
    The things that are more excellent.

To dress, to call, to dine, to break
    No canon of the social code,
The little laws that lacqueys make,
    The futile decalogue of Mode,—
How many a soul for these things lives,
    With pious passion, grave intent !
While Nature careless-handed gives
    The things that are more excellent.

To hug the wealth ye cannot use,
    And lack the riches all may gain,—
O blind and wanting wit to choose,
    Who house the chaff and burn the grain !

And still doth life with starry towers
    Lure to the bright, divine ascent !—
Be yours the things ye would : be ours
    The things that are more excellent.

The grace of friendship—mind and heart
    Linked with their fellow heart and mind
The gains of science, gifts of art ;
    The sense of oneness with our kind ;
The thirst to know and understand—
    A large and liberal discontent :
These are the goods in life's rich hand,
    The things that are more excellent.

In faultless rhythm the ocean rolls,
    A rapturous silence thrills the skies ;
And on this earth are lovely souls,
    That softly look with aidful eyes.
Though dark, O God, Thy course and track,
    I think Thou must at least have meant
That nought which lives should wholly lack
    The things that are more excellent.

EPIGRAM

IN youth the artist voweth lover's vows
To Art, in manhood maketh her his spouse.
Well if her charms yet hold for him such joy
As when he craved some boon and she was coy!

THE GREAT MISGIVING

"NOT ours," say some, "the thought of death to
    dread ;
  Asking no heaven, we fear no fabled hell :
Life is a feast, and we have banqueted—
  Shall not the worms as well ?

"The after-silence, when the feast is o'er,
  And void the places where the minstrels stood,
Differs in nought from what hath been before,
  And is nor ill nor good."

Ah, but the Apparition—the dumb sign—
  The beckoning finger bidding me forego
The fellowship, the converse, and the wine,
  The songs, the festal glow !

And ah, to know not, while with friends I sit,
   And while the purple joy is passed about,
Whether 'tis ampler day divinelier lit
   Or homeless night without ;

And whether, stepping forth, my soul shall see
   New prospects, or fall sheer—a blinded thing !
There is, O grave, thy hourly victory,
   And there, O death, thy sting.

TO LORD TENNYSON

(With a Volume of Verse)

MASTER and mage, our prince of song, whom Time
In this your autumn mellow and serene,
Crowns ever with fresh laurels, not less green
Than garlands dewy from your verdurous prime;
Heir of the riches of the whole world's rhyme,
Dow'r'd with the Attic grace, the Mantuan mien,
With Arno's depth and Avon's golden sheen;
Singer to whom the singing ages climb,
Convergent;—if the youngest of the choir
May snatch a flying splendour from your name,
Making his page illustrious, and aspire
For one rich moment your regard to claim,
Suffer him at your feet to lay his lyre
And touch the skirts and fringes of your fame.

THE KEY-BOARD

FIVE-AND-THIRTY black slaves,
  Half-a-hundred white,
All their duty but to sing
  For their Queen's delight,
Now with throats of thunder,
  Now with dulcet lips,
While she rules them royally
  With her finger-tips !

When she quits her palace,
  All the slaves are dumb—
Dumb with dolour till the Queen
  Back to Court is come :

THE KEY-BOARD

Dumb the throats of thunder,
  Dumb the dulcet lips,
Lacking all the sovereignty
  Of her finger-tips.

Dusky slaves and pallid,
  Ebon slaves and white,
When the Queen was on her throne
  How you sang to-night !
Ah, the throats of thunder !
  Ah, the dulcet lips !
Ah, the gracious tyrannies
  Of her finger-tips !

Silent, silent, silent,
  All your voices now ;
Was it then her life alone
  Did your life endow ?
Waken, throats of thunder !
  Waken, dulcet lips !
Touched to immortality
  By her finger-tips.

85

AFTER READING "TAMBURLAINE THE GREAT"

YOUR Marlowe's page I close, my Shakespeare's
    ope.
  How welcome—after gong and cymbal's din—
The continuity, the long slow slope
    And vast curves of the gradual violin!

TO A FRIEND

CHAFING AT ENFORCED IDLENESS FROM
INTERRUPTED HEALTH

SOON may the edict lapse, that on you lays

This dire compulsion of infertile days,

This hardest penal toil, reluctant rest!

Meanwhile I count you eminently blest,

Happy from labours heretofore well done,

Happy in tasks auspiciously begun.

For they are blest that have not much to rue—

That have not oft mis-heard the prompter's cue,

Stammered and stumbled and the wrong parts
    played

And life a Tragedy of Errors made.

EPIGRAM

TO keep in sight Perfection, and adore
 The vision, is the artist's best delight;
His bitterest pang, that he can ne'er do more
 Than keep her long'd-for loveliness in sight.

SONNETS

FROM

"VER TENEBROSUM"

The eight sonnets here following are from a series of fifteen, arising out of events of March and April, 1885, and originally published in June of that year.

THE SOUDANESE

THEY wrong'd not us, nor sought 'gainst us to
    wage
The bitter battle.   On their God they cried
For succour, deeming justice to abide
In heaven, if banish'd from earth's vicinage.
And when they rose with a gall'd lion's rage,
We, on the captor's, keeper's, tamer's side,
We, with the alien tyranny allied,
We bade them back to their Egyptian cage.
Scarce knew they who we were !   A wind of blight
From the mysterious far north-west we came.
Our greatness now their veriest babes have learn'd,
Where, in wild desert homes, by day, by night,
Thousands that weep their warriors unreturn'd,
O England, O my country, curse thy name !

THE ENGLISH DEAD

GIVE honour to our heroes fall'n, how ill
Soe'er the cause that bade them forth to die.
Honour to him, the untimely struck, whom high
In place, more high in hope, 'twas fate's harsh
    will
With tedious pain unsplendidly to kill.
Honour to him, doom'd splendidly to die,
Child of the city whose foster-child am I,
Who, hotly leading up the ensanguin'd hill
His charging thousand, fell without a word—
Fell, but shall fall not from our memory.
Also for them let honour's voice be heard
Who nameless sleep, while dull time covereth
With no illustrious shade of laurel tree,
But with the poppy alone, their deeds and death.

RESTORED ALLEGIANCE

DARK is thy trespass, deep be thy remorse,
O England! Fittingly thine own feet bleed,
Submissive to the purblind guides that lead
Thy weary steps along this rugged course.
Yet . . . when I glance abroad, and track the
    source
More selfish far, of other nations' deed,
And mark their tortuous craft, their jealous greed,
Their serpent-wisdom or mere soulless force,
Homeward returns my vagrant fealty,
Crying, "O England, shouldst thou one day fall,
Shatter'd in ruins by some Titan foe,
Justice were thenceforth weaker throughout all
The world, and Truth less passionately free,
And God the poorer for thine overthrow."

GORDON

ARAB, Egyptian, English—by the sword
Cloven, or pierced with spears, or bullet-mown—
In equal fate they sleep ; their dust is grown
A portion of the fiery sands abhorred.
And thou, what hast thou, hero, for reward,
Thou, England's glory and her shame?   O'er-
    thrown
Thou liest, unburied, or with grave unknown
As his to whom on Nebo's height the Lord
Showed all the land of Gilead, unto Dan ;
Judah sea-fringed ; Manasseh and Ephraim ;
And Jericho palmy, to where Zoar lay ;
And in a valley of Moab buried him,
Over against Beth-Peor, but no man
Knows of his sepulchre unto this day.

FOREIGN MENACE

I MARVEL that this land, whereof I claim
The glory of sonship—for it *was* erewhile
A glory to be sprung of Britain's isle,
Though now it well-nigh more resembles shame—
I marvel that this land with heart so tame
Can brook the northern insolence and guile.
But most it angers me, to think how vile
Art thou, how base, from whom the insult
    came,
Unwieldy laggard, many an age behind
Thy sister Powers, in brain and conscience both ;
In recognition of man's widening mind
And flexile adaptation to its growth :
Brute bulk, that bearest on thy back, half loth,
One wretched man, most pitied of mankind.

HOME-ROOTEDNESS

I CANNOT boast myself cosmopolite;
I own to "insularity," although
'Tis fall'n from fashion, as full well I know.
For somehow, being a plain and simple wight,
I am skin-deep a child of the new light,
But chiefly am mere Englishman below,
Of island-fostering; and can hate a foe,
And trust my kin before the Muscovite.
Whom shall I trust if not my kin?   And whom
Account so near in natural bonds as these
Born of my mother England's mighty womb,
Nursed on my mother England's mighty knees,
And lull'd as I was lull'd in glory and gloom
With cradle-song of her protecting seas?

OUR EASTERN TREASURE

IN cobwebb'd corners dusty and dim I hear
A thin voice pipingly revived of late,
Which saith our India is a cumbrous weight,
An idle decoration, bought too dear.
The wiser world contemns not gorgeous gear;
Just pride is no mean factor in a State;
The sense of greatness keeps a nation great;
And mighty they who mighty can appear.
It may be that if hands of greed could steal
From England's grasp the envied orient prize,
This tide of gold would flood her still as now:
But were she the same England, made to feel
A brightness gone from out those starry eyes,
A splendour from that constellated brow?

NIGHTMARE

(Written during apparent Imminence of War)

IN a false dream I saw the Foe prevail.
The war was ended; the last smoke had rolled
Away: and we, erewhile the strong and bold,
Stood broken, humbled, withered, weak and pale,
And moan'd, "Our greatness is become a tale
To tell our children's babes when we are old.
They shall put by their playthings to be told
How England once, before the years of bale,
Throned above trembling, puissant, grandiose, calm,
Held Asia's richest jewel in her palm;
And with unnumbered isles barbaric, she
The broad hem of her glistering robe impearl'd;
Then, when she wound her arms about the world,
And had for vassal the obsequious sea."

A R T

THE thousand painful steps at last are trod,
   At last the temple's difficult door we win;
But perfect on his pedestal, the god
   Freezes us hopeless when we enter in.

THE LUTE-PLAYER

SHE was a lady great and splendid,
  I was a minstrel in her halls.
A warrior like a prince attended
  Stayed his steed by the castle walls.

Far had he fared to gaze upon her.
  "O rest thee now, Sir Knight," she said.
The warrior wooed, the warrior won her,
  In time of snowdrops they were wed.
I made sweet music in his honour,
  And longed to strike him dead.

I passed at midnight from her portal:
  Throughout the world till death I rove:
Ah, let me make this lute immortal
  With rapture of my hate and love!

BEAUTY'S METEMPSYCHOSIS

THAT beauty such as thine
    Should die indeed,
Were ordinance too wantonly malign !
No wit may reconcile so cold a creed
    With beauty such as thine.

From wave and star and flower
    Some effluence rare
Was lent thee, a divine but transient dower :
Thou yield'st it back from eyes and lips and hair
    To wave and star and flower.

Shouldst thou to-morrow die,
    Thou still shalt be
Found in the rose and met in all the sky :
And from the ocean's heart shalt sing to me,
    Shouldst thou to-morrow die.

RELUCTANT SUMMER

RELUCTANT Summer! once, a maid
  Full easy of access,
In many a bee-frequented shade
  Thou didst thy lover bless.
Divinely unreproved I played,
  Then, with each liberal tress —
And art thou grown at last afraid
  Of some too close caress?

Or deem'st that if thou shouldst abide
  My passion might decay?
Thou leav'st me pining and denied,
  Coyly thou say'st me nay.
Ev'n as I woo thee to my side,
  Thou, importuned to stay,
Like Orpheus' half-recovered bride
  Ebb'st from my arms away.

KEATS

HE dwelt with the bright gods of elder time,
  On earth and in their cloudy haunts above.
He loved them : and in recompense sublime,
  The gods, alas ! gave him their fatal love.

AT THE GRAVE OF CHARLES LAMB,
IN EDMONTON

NOT here, O teeming City, was it meet
Thy lover, thy most faithful, should repose,
But where the multitudinous life-tide flows
Whose ocean-murmur was to him more sweet
Than melody of birds at morn, or bleat
Of flocks in Spring-time, *there* should Earth enclose
His earth, amid thy thronging joys and woes,
There, 'neath the music of thy million feet.
In love of thee this lover knew no peer.
Thine eastern or thy western fane had made
Fit habitation for his noble shade.
Mother of mightier far, of none more dear,
Not here, in rustic exile, O not here,
Thy Elia like an alien should be laid!

TO AUSTIN DOBSON

YES! urban is your Muse, and owns
An empire based on London stones;
Yet flow'rs, as mountain violets sweet,
Spring from the pavement 'neath her feet.

Of wilder birth this Muse of mine,
Hill-cradled, and baptized with brine;
And 'tis for her a sweet despair
To watch that courtly step and air!

Yet surely she, without reproof,
Greeting may send from realms aloof,
And even claim a tie in blood,
And dare to deem it sisterhood.

TO AUSTIN DOBSON

For well we know, those Maidens be
All daughters of Mnemosyne ;
And 'neath the unifying sun,
Many the songs—but Song is one.

LINES IN A FLYLEAF OF
"CHRISTABEL"

INHOSPITABLY hast thou entertained,

O Poet, us the bidden to thy board,

Whom in mid-feast, and while our thousand
    mouths

Are one laudation of the festal cheer,

Thou from thy table dost dismiss, unfilled.

Yet loudlier thee than many a lavish host

We praise, and oftener thy repast half-served

Than many a stintless banquet, prodigally

Through satiate hours prolonged; nor praise less
    well

Because with tongues thou hast not cloyed, and lips

That mourn the parsimony of affluent souls,

And mix the lamentation with the laud.

A GOLDEN HOUR

A BECKONING spirit of gladness seemed afloat,
  That lightly danced in laughing air before us :
The earth was all in tune, and you a note
    Of Nature's happy chorus.

'Twas like a vernal morn, yet overhead
  The leafless boughs across the lane were knitting :
The ghost of some forgotten Spring, we said,
    O'er Winter's world comes flitting.

Or was it Spring herself, that, gone astray,
  Beyond the alien frontier chose to tarry ?
Or but some bold outrider of the May,
    Some April-emissary ?

A GOLDEN HOUR

The apparition faded on the air,
    Capricious and incalculable comer.—
Wilt thou too pass, and leave my chill days bare,
    And fall'n my phantom Summer?

BYRON THE VOLUPTUARY

TOO avid of earth's bliss, he was of those
   Whom Delight flies because they give her chase.
Only the odour of her wild hair blows
   Back in their faces hungering for her face.

THE FUGITIVE IDEAL.

AS some most pure and noble face,
　　Seen in the thronged and hurrying street,
Sheds o'er the world a sudden grace,
　　　A flying odour sweet,
Then, passing, leaves the cheated sense
Baulked with a phantom excellence;

So, on our souls the visions rise
　　Of that fair life we never led:
They flash a splendour past our eyes,
　　　We start, and they are fled:
They pass, and leave us with blank gaze,
Resigned to our ignoble days.

COLUMBUS

FROM his adventurous prime
He dreamed the dream sublime:
  Over his wandering youth
    It hung, a beckoning star.
At last the vision fled,
And left him in its stead
  The scarce sublimer truth,
    The world he found afar.

The scattered isles that stand
Warding the mightier land
  Yielded their maidenhood
    To his imperious prow.

COLUMBUS

The mainland within call
Lay vast and virginal :
   In its blue porch he stood :
     No more did fate allow.

No more ! but ah, how much,
To be the first to touch
   The veriest azure hem
     Of that majestic robe !
Lord of the lordly sea,
Earth's mightiest sailor he :
   Great Captain among them,
     The captors of the globe.

When shall the world forget
Thy glory and our debt,
   Indomitable soul,
     Immortal Genoese ?
Not while the shrewd salt gale
Whines amid shroud and sail,
   Above the rhythmic roll
     And thunder of the seas.

H

TO JAMES BROMLEY

With "Wordsworth's Grave"

ERE vandal lords with lust of gold accurst
  Deface each hallowed hillside we revere—
Ere cities in their million-throated thirst
  Menace each sacred mere—
Let us give thanks because one nook hath been
  Unflooded yet by desecration's wave,
The little churchyard in the valley green
  That holds our Wordsworth's grave.

'Twas there I plucked these elegiac blooms,
  There where he rests 'mid comrades fit and few,
And thence I bring this growth of classic tombs,
  An offering, friend, to you--

TO JAMES BROMLEY

You who have loved like me his simple themes,
    Loved his sincere large accent nobly plain,
And loved the land whose mountains and whose
        streams
    Are lovelier for his strain.

It may be that his manly chant, beside
    More dainty numbers, seems a rustic tune;
It may be, thought has broadened since he
        died
    Upon the century's noon;
It may be that we can no longer share
    The faith which from his fathers he received;
It may be that our doom is to despair
    Where he with joy believed;--

Enough that there is none since risen who
        sings
    A song so gotten of the immediate soul,
So instant from the vital fount of things
    Which is our source and goal;

And though at touch of later hands there float
  More artful tones than from his lyre he
    drew,
Ages may pass ere trills another note
  So sweet, so great, so true.

THE SAINT AND THE SATYR

(Mediæval Legend)

SAINT ANTHONY the eremite
    He wandered in the wold,
And there he saw a hoofèd wight
    That blew his hands for cold.

"What dost thou here in misery,
    That better far wert dead?"
The eremite Saint Anthony
    Unto the Satyr said.

"Lorn in the wold," the thing replied,
    "I sit and make my moan,
For all the gods I loved have died,
    And I am left alone.

THE SAINT AND THE SATYR

"Silent in Paphos Venus sleeps,
    And Jove on Ida mute;
And every living creature weeps
    Pan and his perished flute.

"The Faun, his laughing heart is broke;
    The nymph, her fountain fails;
And driven from out the hollow oak
    The Hamadryad wails.

"A God more beautiful than mine
    Hath conquered mine, they say.—
Ah, to that fair young God of thine,
    For me I pray thee pray!"

THY voice from inmost dreamland calls
  The wastes of sleep thou makest fair;
Bright o'er the ridge of darkness falls
  The cataract of thy hair.

The morn renews its golden birth:
  Thou with the vanquished night dost fade;
And leav'st the ponderable earth
  Less real than thy shade.

THE CATHEDRAL SPIRE

IT soars like hearts of hapless men who dare
　To sue for gifts the gods refuse to allot ;
Who climb for ever toward they know not where,
　Baffled for ever by they know not what.

A DEDICATION

(To London, my Hostess)

CITY that waitest to be sung,—
   For whom no hand
To mighty strains the lyre hath strung
   In all this land,
Though mightier theme the mightiest ones
   Sang not of old,
The thrice three sisters' godlike sons
   With lips of gold,—
Till greater voice thy greatness sing
   In loftier times,
Suffer an alien muse to bring
   Her votive rhymes.

A DEDICATION

Yes, alien in thy midst am I,
  Not of thy brood ;
The nursling of a norland sky
  Of rougher mood :
To me, thy tarrying guest, to me,
  'Mid thy loud hum,
Strayed visions of the moor or sea
  Tormenting come.

Above the thunder of the wheels
  That hurry by,
From lapping of lone waves there steals
  A far-sent sigh ;
And many a dream-reared mountain crest
  My feet have trod,
There where thy Minster in the West
  Gropes toward God.

Yet, from thy presence if I go,
  By woodlands deep
Or ocean-fringes, thou, I know,
  Wilt haunt my sleep ;
Thy restless tides of life will foam,
  Still, in my sight ;

A DEDICATION

Thy imperturbable dark dome
    Will crown my night.

O sea of living waves that roll
    On golden sands,
Or break on tragic reef and shoal
    'Mid fatal lands;
O forest wrought of living leaves,
    Some filled with Spring,
Where joy life's festal raiment weaves
    And all birds sing, -
Some trampled in the miry ways,
    Or whirled along
By fury of tempestuous days,—
    Take thou my song!

For thou hast scorned not heretofore
    The gifts of rhyme
I dropped, half faltering, at thy door,
    City sublime;

A DEDICATION

And though 'tis true I am but guest
    Within thy gate,
Unto thy hands I owe the best
    Awards of fate.
Imperial hostess! thanks from me
    To thee belong:
O living forest, living sea,
    Take thou my song!

THE DREAM OF MAN

TO the eye and the ear of the Dreamer this Dream
 out of darkness flew,
Through the horn or the ivory portal, but he wist
 not which of the two.

It was the Human Spirit, of all men's souls the Soul,
Man the unwearied climber, that climbed to the
 unknown goal.
And up the steps of the ages, the difficult steep ascent,
Man the unwearied climber pauseless and dauntless
 went.
Æons rolled behind him with thunder of far retreat,
And still as he strove he conquered and laid his foes
 at his feet.
Inimical powers of nature, tempest and flood and fire,

The spleen of fickle seasons that loved to baulk his
  desire,

The breath of hostile climates, the ravage of blight
  and dearth,

The old unrest that vexes the heart of the moody
  earth,

The genii swift and radiant sabreing heaven with
  flame,

He, with a keener weapon, the sword of his wit,
  overcame.

Disease and her ravening offspring, pain with the
  thousand teeth,

He drave into night primeval, the nethermost worlds
  beneath,

Till the Lord of Death, the undying, ev'n Asraël the
  King,

No more with Furies for heralds came armed with
  scourge and sting,

But gentle of voice and of visage, by calm Age
  ushered and led,

A guest, serenely featured, entering, woke no dread.

And, as the rolling æons retreated with pomp of sound,

Man's Spirit, grown too lordly for this mean orb to
    bound,
By arts in his youth undreamed of his terrene fetters
    broke,
With enterprise ethereal spurning the natal yoke,
And, stung with divine ambition, and fired with a
    glorious greed,
He annexed the stars and the planets and peopled
    them with his seed.

Then said he, "The infinite Scripture I have read
    and interpreted clear,
And searching all worlds I have found not my
    sovereign or my peer.
In what room of the palace of nature resides the
    invisible God?
For all her doors I have opened, and all her floors I
    have trod.
If greater than I be her tenant, let him answer my
    challenging call:
Till then I admit no rival, but crown myself master
    of all."

And forth as that word went bruited, by Man unto
Man were raised

Fanes of devout self-homage, where he who praised
was the praised ;

And from vast unto vast of creation the new evangel
ran,

And an odour of world-wide incense went up from
Man unto Man ;

Until, on a solemn feast-day, when the world's
usurping lord

At a million impious altars his own proud image
adored,

God spake as He stept from His ambush : " O great
in thine own conceit,

I will show thee thy source, how humble, thy goal,
for a god how unmeet."

Thereat, by the word of the Maker the Spirit of
Man was led

To a mighty peak of vision, where God to His
creature said :

THE DREAM OF MAN

"Look eastward toward time's sunrise." And, age
    upon age untold,
The Spirit of Man saw clearly the Past as a chart
    out-rolled,—
Beheld his base beginnings in the depths of time,
    and his strife
With beasts and crawling horrors for leave to live,
    when life
Meant but to slay and to procreate, to feed and to
    sleep, among
Mere mouths, voracities boundless, blind lusts,
    desires without tongue,
And ferocities vast, fulfilling their being's malignant
    law,
While nature was one hunger, and one hate, all
    fangs and maw.

With that, for a single moment, abashed at his own
    descent,
In humbleness Man's Spirit at the feet of the Maker
    bent:

But, swifter than light, he recovered the stature and
    pose of his pride,

And, "Think not thus to shame me with my mean
    birth," he cried.

"This is my loftiest greatness, to have been born so
    low ;

Greater than Thou the ungrowing am I that for
    ever grow."

And God forbore to rebuke him, but answered
    brief and stern,

Bidding him toward time's sunset his vision west-
    ward turn ;

And the Spirit of Man obeying beheld as a chart
    out-rolled

The likeness and form of the Future, age upon age
    untold ;

Beheld his own meridian, and beheld his dark decline,

His secular fall to nadir from summits of light divine,

Till at last, amid worlds exhausted, and bankrupt
    of force and fire,

'Twas his, in a torrent of darkness, like a sputtering
    lamp to expire.

Then a war of shame and anger did the realm of
  his soul divide;

" 'Tis false, 'tis a lying vision," in the face of his
  God he cried.

"Thou thinkest to daunt me with shadows; not
  such as Thou feign'st, my doom:

From glory to rise unto glory is mine, who have
  risen from gloom.

I doubt if Thou knew'st at my making how near to
  Thy throne I should climb,

O'er the mountain slopes of the ages and the
  conquered peaks of time.

Nor shall I look backward nor rest me till the
  uttermost heights I have trod,

And am equalled with Thee or above Thee, the
  mate or the master of God."

Ev'n thus Man turned from the Maker, with
  thundered defiance wild,

And God with a terrible silence reproved the speech
  of His child.

And Man returned to his labours, and stiffened the
neck of his will;

And the æons still went rolling, and his power was
crescent still.

But yet there remained to conquer one foe, and
the greatest—although

Despoiled of his ancient terrors, at heart, as of old,
a foe—

Unmaker of all, and renewer, who winnows the
world with his wing,

The Lord of Death, the undying, ev'n Asraël the
King.

And lo, Man mustered his forces the war of wars to
wage,

And with storm and thunder of onset did the foe of
foes engage,

And the Lord of Death, the undying, was beset and
harried sore,

In his immemorial fastness at night's aboriginal core.

And during years a thousand man leaguered his
enemy's hold,

While nature was one deep tremor, and the heart of
    the world waxed cold,

Till the phantom battlements wavered, and the
    ghostly fortress fell,

And Man with shadowy fetters bound fast great
    Asraël.

So, to each star in the heavens, the exultant word
    was blown,

The annunciation tremendous, *Death is overthrown !*

And Space in her ultimate borders, prolonging the
    jubilant tone,

With hollow ingeminations, sighed, *Death is over-*
    thrown !

And God in His house of silence, where He
    dwelleth aloof, alone,

Paused in His tasks to hearken : *Death is overthrown !*

Then a solemn and high thanksgiving by Man unto
    Man was sung,

In his temples of self-adoration, with his own multi-
    tudinous tongue ;

And he said to his Soul: "Rejoice thou, for thy last
  great foe lies bound,
Ev'n Asraël the Unmaker, unmade, disarmed,
  discrowned."

And behold, his Soul rejoiced not, the breath of
  whose being was strife,
For life with nothing to vanquish seemed but the
  shadow of life.
No goal invited and promised and divinely provoca-
  tive shone;
And Fear having fled, her sister, blest Hope, in her
  train was gone;
And the coping and crown of achievement was hell
  than defeat more dire—
The torment of all-things-compassed, the plague of
  nought-to-desire;
And Man the invincible queller, man with his foot
  on his foes,
In boundless satiety hungered, restless from utter
  repose,

Victor of nature, victor of the prince of the powers
of the air,

By mighty weariness vanquished, and crowned with
august despair.

Then, at his dreadful zenith, he cried unto God:
"O Thou

Whom of old in my days of striving methought I
needed not,—now

In this my abject glory, my hopeless and helpless
might,

Hearken and cheer and succour!" and God from
His lonely height,

From eternity's passionless summits, on suppliant
Man looked down,

And his brow waxed human with pity, belying its
awful crown.

"Thy richest possession," He answered, "blest
Hope, will I restore,

And the infinite wealth of weakness which was thy
strength of yore;

135

And I will arouse from slumber, in his hold where
bound he lies,

Thine enemy most benefic;—O Asraël, hear and
rise!"

And a sound like the heart of nature in sunder
cloven and torn,

Announced, to the ear universal, undying Death
new-born.

Sublime he rose in his fetters, and shook the chains
aside

Ev'n as some mortal sleeper 'mid forests in autumn-
tide

Rises and shakes off lightly the leaves that lightly
fell

On his limbs and his hair unheeded while as yet
he slumbered well.

And Deity paused and hearkened, then turned to
the undivine,

Saying, "O Man, My creature, thy lot was more
blest than Mine.

I taste not delight of seeking, nor the boon of
  longing know.
There is but one joy transcendent, and I hoard it
  not but bestow.
I hoard it not nor have tasted, but freely I gave it
  to thee—
The joy of most glorious striving, which dieth in
  victory."

Thus, to the Soul of the Dreamer, this Dream out
  of darkness flew,
Through the horn or the ivory portal, but he wist
  not which of the two.

TOILING and yearning, 'tis man's doom to see
  No perfect creature fashion'd of his hands.
Insulted by a flower's immaculacy,
  And mock'd at by the flawless stars he stands.

VITA NUOVA

VITA NUOVA

LONG hath she slept, forgetful of delight :
At last, at last, the enchanted princess, Earth,
Claimed with a kiss by Spring the adventurer,
In slumber knows the destined lips, and thrilled
Through all the deeps of her imageing heart
With passionate necessity of joy,
Wakens, and yields her loveliness to love.

O ancient streams, O far-descended woods
Full of the fluttering of melodious souls;
O hills and valleys that adorn yourselves
In solemn jubilation ; winds and clouds,
Ocean and land in stormy nuptials clasped,
And all exuberant creatures that acclaim
The Earth's divine renewal : lo, I too

VITA NUOVA

With yours would mingle somewhat of glad song.

I too have come through wintry terrors,—yea,

Through tempest and through cataclysm of soul

Have come, and am delivered.   Me the Spring,

Me also, dimly with new life hath touched,

And with regenerate hope, the salt of life ;

And I would dedicate these thankful tears

To whatsoever Power beneficent,

Veiled though his countenance, undivulged his
   thought,

Hath led me from the haunted darkness forth

Into the gracious air and vernal morn,

And suffers me to know my spirit a note

Of this great chorus, one with bird and stream

And voiceful mountain,—nay, a string, how jarred

And all but broken ! of that lyre of life

Whereon himself, the master harp-player,

Resolving all its mortal dissonance

To one immortal and most perfect strain,

Harps without pause, building with song the world.

18th March 1895.

THE FIRST SKYLARK OF SPRING

TWO worlds hast thou to dwell in, Sweet,—
   The virginal, untroubled sky,
And this vext region at my feet.—
    Alas, but one have I !

To all my songs there clings the shade,
   The dulling shade, of mundane care.
They amid mortal mists are made,—
    Thine, in immortal air.

My heart is dashed with griefs and fears ;
   My song comes fluttering, and is gone.
O high above the home of tears,
    Eternal Joy, sing on !

141

THE FIRST SKYLARK OF SPRING

Not loftiest bard, of mightiest mind,
   Shall ever chant a note so pure,
Till he can cast this earth behind
   And breathe in heaven secure.

We sing of Life, with stormy breath
   That shakes the lute's distempered string:
We sing of Love, and loveless Death
   Takes up the song we sing.

And born in toils of Fate's control,
   Insurgent from the womb, we strive
With proud, unmanumitted soul
   To burst the golden gyve.

Thy spirit knows nor bounds nor bars;
   On thee no shreds of thraldom hang:
Not more enlarged, the morning stars
   Their great Te Deum sang.

THE FIRST SKYLARK OF SPRING

But I am fettered to the sod,
 And but forget my bonds an hour :
In amplitude of dreams a god,
 A slave in dearth of power.

And fruitless knowledge clouds my soul,
 And fretful ignorance irks it more.
Thou sing'st as if thou knew'st the whole,
 And lightly held'st thy lore !

Somewhat as thou, Man once could sing,
 In porches of the lucent morn,
Ere he had felt his lack of wing,
 Or cursed his iron bourn.

The springtime bubbled in his throat,
 The sweet sky seemed not far above,
And young and lovesome came the note ;—
 Ah, thine is Youth and Love !

THE FIRST SKYLARK OF SPRING

Thou sing'st of what he knew of old,
    And dreamlike from afar recalls;
In flashes of forgotten gold
    An orient glory falls.

And as he listens, one by one
    Life's utmost splendours blaze more nigh;
Less inaccessible the sun,
    Less alien grows the sky.

For thou art native to the spheres,
    And of the courts of heaven art free,
And carriest to his temporal ears
    News from eternity;

And lead'st him to the dizzy verge,
    And lur'st him o'er the dazzling line,
Where mortal and immortal merge,
    And human dies divine.

NIGHT ON CURBAR EDGE

NO echo of man's life pursues my ears;
Nothing disputes this Desolation's reign;
Change comes not, this dread temple to profane,
Where time by æons reckons, not by years.
Its patient form one crag, sole stranded, rears,
Type of whate'er is destined to remain
While you still host encamped on night's waste plain
Keeps armèd watch, a million quivering spears.

Hushed are the wild and wing'd lives of the moor:
The sleeping sheep nestle 'neath ruined wall,
Or unhewn stones in random concourse hurled:
Solitude, sleepless, listens at Fate's door;
And there is built and 'stablisht over all
Tremendous silence, older than the world.

EPIGRAM

IF Nature be a phantasm, as thou say'st,
  A splendid fiction and prodigious dream,
To reach the real and true I'll make no haste,
  More than content with worlds that only seem.

ODE TO LICINIUS

(Horace II. x.)

LICINIUS, wouldst thou wisely steer
  The pinnace of thy soul,
Not always trust her without fear
  Where deep-sea billows roll;
Nor, to the sheltered beach too near,
  Risk shipwreck on the shoal.

Who sees in fortune's golden mean
  All his desires comprised,
Midway the cot and court between
  Hath well his life devised;
For riches, hath not envied been,
  Nor, for their lack, despised.

ODE TO LICINIUS

Most rocks the pine that soars afar,
  When leaves are tempest-whirled.
Direst the crash when turrets are
  In dusty ruin hurled.
The thunder loveth best to scar
  The bright brows of the world.

The steadfast mind, that to the end
  Is fortune's victor still,
Hath yet a fear, though Fate befriend
  A hope, though all seem ill.
Jove can at will the winter send,
  Or call the spring at will.

Full oft the darkest day may be
  Of morrows bright the sire.
His bow not everlastingly
  Apollo bends in ire.
At times the silent Muses he
  Wakes with his dulcet lyre.

ODE TO LICINIUS

When life's straits roar and hem thee sore,
    Be bold; naught else avails.
But when thy canvas swells before
    Too proudly prospering gales,
For once be wise with coward's lore,
    And timely reef thy sails.

HERE love the slain with Love the slayer lies ;
  Deep drown'd are both in the same sunless pool.
Up from its depths that mirror thundering skies
  Bubbles the wan mirth of the mirthless Fool.

TELL ME NOT NOW

TELL me not now, if love for love
    Thou canst return,—
Now while around us and above
    Day's flambeaux burn.
Not in clear noon, with speech as clear,
    Thy heart avow,
For every gossip wind to hear;
    Tell me not now!

Tell me not now the tidings sweet,
    The news divine;
A little longer at thy feet
    Leave me to pine.

TELL ME NOT NOW

I would not have the gadding bird
    Hear from his bough;
Nay, though I famish for a word,
    Tell me not now!

But when deep trances of delight
    All Nature seal,
When round the world the arms of Night
    Caressing steal,
When rose to dreaming rose says, " *Dear,*
    Dearest,"—and when
Heaven sighs her secret in earth's ear,
    Ah, tell me then!

THE FATHER OF THE FOREST

I

OLD emperor Yew, fantastic sire,
    Girt with thy guard of dotard kings,—
What ages hast thou seen retire
    Into the dusk of alien things?
What mighty news hath stormed thy shade,
Of armies perished, realms unmade?

Already wast thou great and wise,
    And solemn with exceeding eld,
On that proud morn when England's eyes,
    Wet with tempestuous joy, beheld
Round her rough coasts the thundering main
Strewn with the ruined dream of Spain.

153

THE FATHER OF THE FOREST

Hardly thou count'st them long ago,
   The warring faiths, the wavering land,
The sanguine sky's delirious glow,
   And Cranmer's scorched, uplifted hand.
Wailed not the woods their task of shame,
Doomed to provide the insensate flame?

Mourned not the rumouring winds, when she,
   The sweet queen of a tragic hour,
Crowned with her snow-white memory
   The crimson legend of the Tower?
Or when a thousand witcheries lay
Felled with one stroke, at Fotheringay?

Ah, thou hast heard the iron tread
   And clang of many an armoured age,
And well recall'st the famous dead,
   Captains or counsellors brave or sage,
Kings that on kings their myriads hurled,
Ladies whose smile embroiled the world.

THE FATHER OF THE FOREST

Rememberest thou the perfect knight,
  The soldier, courtier, bard in one,
Sidney, that pensive Hesper-light
  O'er Chivalry's departed sun?
Knew'st thou the virtue, sweetness, lore,
Whose nobly hapless name was More?

The roystering prince, that afterward
  Belied his madcap youth, and proved
A greatly simple warrior lord
  Such as our warrior fathers loved—
Lives he not still? for Shakespeare sings
The last of our adventurer kings.

His battles o'er, he takes his ease,
  Glory put by, and sceptred toil.
Round him the carven centuries
  Like forest branches arch and coil.
In that dim fane, he is not sure
Who lost or won at Azincour!

THE FATHER OF THE FOREST

Roofed by the mother minster vast
    That guards Augustine's rugged throne,
The darling of a knightly Past
    Sleeps in his bed of sculptured stone,
And flings, o'er many a warlike tale,
The shadow of his dusky mail.

The monarch who, albeit his crown
    Graced an august and sapient head,
Rode roughshod to a stained renown
    O'er Wallace and Llewellyn dead,
And perished in the hostile land,
With restless heart and ruthless hand;

Or that disastrous king on whom
    Fate, like a tempest, early fell.
And the dark secret of whose doom
    The Keep of Pomfret kept full well:
Or him that with half careless words
On Becket drew the dastard swords:

Or Eleanor's undaunted son,
 That, starred with idle glory, came
Bearing from leaguered Ascalon
 The barren splendour of his fame,
And, vanquished by an unknown bow,
Lies vainly great at Fontevraud;

Or him, the footprints of whose power
 Made mightier whom he overthrew:
A man built like a mountain-tower,
 A fortress of heroic thew;
The Conqueror, in our soil who set
This stem of Kinghood flowering yet;

These, or the living fame of these,
 Perhaps thou minglest—who shall say?—
With thrice remoter memories,
 And phantoms of the mistier day,
Long ere the tanner's daughter's son
From Harold's hands this realm had won.

THE FATHER OF THE FOREST

What years are thine, not mine to guess!
   The stars look youthful, thou being by;
Youthful the sun's glad-heartedness;
   Witless of time the unageing sky!
And these dim-groping roots around
So deep a human Past are wound,

That, musing in thy shade, for me
   The tidings scarce would strangely fall
Of fair-haired despots of the sea
   Scaling our eastern island-wall,
From their long ships of norland pine,
Their " surf-deer," driven o'er wilds of brine.

Nay, hid by thee from Summer's gaze
   That seeks in vain this couch of loam,
I should behold, without amaze,
   Camped on yon down the hosts of Rome,
Nor start though English woodlands heard
The self-same mandatory word

THE FATHER OF THE FOREST

As by the Cataracts of the Nile
　　Marshalled the legions long ago,
Or where the lakes are one blue smile
　　'Neath pageants of Helvetian snow,
Or 'mid the Syrian sands that lie
Sick of the day's great tearless eye,

Or on barbaric plains afar,
　　Where, under Asia's fevering ray,
The long lines of imperial war
　　O'er Tigris passed, and with dismay
In fanged and iron deserts found
Embattled Persia closing round,

And 'mid their eagles watched on high
　　The vultures gathering for a feast,
Till, from the quivers of the sky,
　　The gorgeous star-flight of the East
Flamed, and the bow of darkness bent
O'er Julian dying in his tent.

II

Was it the wind befooling me
    With ancient echoes, as I lay?
Was it the antic fantasy
    Whose elvish mockeries cheat the day?
Surely a hollow murmur stole
From wizard bough and ghostly bole:

" Who prates to me of arms and kings,
    Here in these courts of old repose?
Thy babble is of transient things,
    Broils, and the dust of foolish blows.
Thy sounding annals are at best
The witness of a world's unrest.

" Goodly the ostents are to thee,
    And pomps of Time: to me more sweet
The vigils of Eternity,
    And Silence patient at my feet,
And dreams beyond the deadening range
And dull monotonies of Change.

" Often an air comes idling by
   With news of cities and of men.
I hear a multitudinous sigh,
   And lapse into my soul again.
Shall her great noons and sunsets be
Blurred with thine infelicity ?

" Now from these veins the strength of old,
   The warmth and lust of life depart ;
Full of mortality, behold
   The cavern that was once my heart !
Me, with blind arm, in season due,
Let the aërial woodman hew.

" For not though mightiest mortals fall,
   The starry chariot hangs delayed.
His axle is uncooled, nor shall
   The thunder of His wheels be stayed.
A changeless pace His coursers keep,
And halt not at the wells of sleep.

" The South shall bless, the East shall blight,
    The red rose of the Dawn shall blow ;
The million-lilied stream of Night
    Wide in ethereal meadows flow ;
And Autumn mourn ; and everything
Dance to the wild pipe of the Spring.

" With oceans heedless round her feet,
    And the indifferent heavens above,
Earth shall the ancient tale repeat
    Of wars and tears, and death and love ;
And, wise from all the foolish Past,
Shall peradventure hail at last

" The advent of that morn divine
    When nations may as forests grow,
Wherein the oak hates not the pine,
    Nor beeches wish the cedars woe,
But all, in their unlikeness, blend
Confederate to one golden end—

" Beauty : the Vision whereunto,
    In joy, with pantings, from afar,
Through sound and odour, form and hue,
    And mind and clay, and worm and star—
Now touching goal, now backward hurled—
Toils the indomitable world."

MOMENTOUS to himself as I to me
    Hath each man been that ever woman bore;
Once, in a lightning-flash of sympathy,
    I *felt* this truth, an instant, and no more.

LINES WRITTEN IN RICHMOND PARK

LADY, were you but here !
The Autumn flames away,
And pensive in the antlered shade I stray.
The Autumn flames away, his end is near.
I linger where deposed and fall'n he lies,
Prankt in his last poor tattered braveries,
And think what brightness would enhance the Day,
Lady, were you but here.
Though hushed the woodlands, though sedate the
     skies,
Though dank the leaves and sere,
The storèd sunlight in your hair and eyes
Would vernalise
November, and renew the agèd year,
Lady ! were you but here.

THE SOVEREIGN POET

HE sits above the clang and dust of Time,
With the world's secret trembling on his lip.
He asks not converse nor companionship
In the cold starlight where thou canst not climb.

   The undelivered tidings in his breast
Suffer him not to rest.
He sees afar the immemorable throng,
And binds the scattered ages with a song.

   The glorious riddle of his rhythmic breath,
His might, his spell, we know not what they be:
We only feel, whate'er he uttereth,
This savours not of death,
This hath a relish of eternity.

THE RUINED ABBEY

FLOWER - FONDLED, clasp'd in ivy's close
    caress,
  It seems allied with Nature, yet apart :—
Of wood's and wave's insensate loveliness
  The glad, sad, tranquil, passionate, human heart.

SONNET

I THINK you never were of earthly frame,
O truant from some charmèd world unknown !
A fairy empress, you forsook your throne,
Fled your inviolate court, and hither came ;
Donned mortal vesture ; wore a woman's name ;
Like a mere woman, loved ; and so are grown
At last a little human, save alone
For the wild elvish heart not Love could tame.
And one day I believe you will return
To your far isle amid the enchanted sea,—
There, in your realm, perhaps remember me,
Perhaps forget : but I shall never learn !
I, loveless dust within a dreamless urn,
Dead to your beauty's immortality.

ODE TO ARTHUR CHRISTOPHER BENSON

IN that grave shade august
 That round your Eton clings,
To you the centuries must
 Be visible corporate things,
And the high Past appear
Affably real and near,
For all its grandiose airs, caught from the mien of
 Kings.

The new age stands as yet
 Half built against the sky,
Open to every threat
 Of storms that clamour by:
Scaffolding veils the walls,
And dim dust floats and falls,
As, moving to and fro, their tasks the masons ply.

But changeless and complete,
　　Rise unperturbed and vast,
Above our din and heat,
　　The turrets of the Past,
Mute as that city asleep,
Lulled with enchantments deep,
Far in Arabian dreamland built where all things
　　　　last.

Who loves not to explore
　　That palace of Old Time,
Awed by the spires that soar
　　In ghostly dusk sublime,
And gorgeous-windowed halls,
And leagues of pictured walls,
And dungeons that remember many a crimson
　　　　crime?

Yet, in those phantom towers
　　Not thine, not mine, to dwell,
Rapt from the living hours
　　By some rich lotus-spell;

And if our lute obey
A mode of yesterday,
'Tis that we deem 'twill prove to-morrow's mode
as well.

This neighbouring joy and woe –
This present sky and sea—
These men and things we know,
Whose touch we would not flee—
To us, O friend, shall long
Yield aliment of song :
Life as I see it lived is great enough for me.

In high relief against
That reverend silence set,
Wherein your days are fenced
From the world's peevish fret,
There breaks on old Earth's ears
The thunder of new years,
Rousing from ancient dreams the Muse's anchoret.

Well if the coming time,
   With loud and strident tongue,
Hush not the sound of rhyme,
   Drown not the song half sung,
Ev'n as a dissonant age
Choked with polemic rage
The starriest voice that e'er on English ears hath
     rung,

And bade her seer a while
   Pause and put by the bard,
Till this tormented isle,
   With feuds and factions jarred,
Some leisure might regain
To hear the long-pent strain
Re-risen from storm and fire, immortal and un-
     marred.

HYMN TO THE SEA

I

GRANT, O regal in bounty, a subtle and delicate
largess;
  Grant an ethereal alms, out of the wealth of thy
  soul:
Suffer a tarrying minstrel, who finds, not fashions
  his numbers,—
  Who, from the commune of air, cages the volatile
  song,—
Here to capture and prison some fugitive breath
  of thy descant,
  Thine and his own as thy roar lisped on the
  lips of a shell,

173

Now while the vernal impulsion makes lyrical all
    that hath language,
  While, through the veins of the Earth, riots the
    ichor of Spring,
While, with throes, with raptures, with loosing of
    bonds, with unsealings,—
  Arrowy pangs of delight, piercing the core of
    the world,—
Tremors and coy unfoldings, reluctances, sweet
    agitations,—
  Youth, irrepressibly fair, wakes like a wondering
    rose.

II

Lover whose vehement kisses on lips irresponsive
    are squandered,
  Lover that wooest in vain Earth's imperturbable
    heart;
Athlete mightily frustrate, who pittest thy thews
    against legions,
  Locked with fantastical hosts, bodiless arms of
    the sky;

Sea that breakest for ever, that breakest and never
    art broken,
  Like unto thine, from of old, springeth the spirit
    of man,--

Nature's wooer and fighter, whose years are a suit
    and a wrestling,
  All their hours, from his birth, hot with desire
    and with fray;

Amorist agonist man, that, immortally pining and
    striving,
  Snatches the glory of life only from love and
    from war;

Man that, rejoicing in conflict, like thee when pre-
    cipitate tempest,
  Charge after thundering charge, clangs on thy
    resonant mail,

Seemeth so easy to shatter, and proveth so hard
    to be cloven;
  Man whom the gods, in his pain, curse with a
    soul that endures;

Man whose deeds, to the doer, come back as thine
    own exhalations

Into thy bosom return, weepings of mountain and
vale ;
Man with the cosmic fortunes and starry vicissitudes
tangled,
Chained to the wheel of the world, blind with
the dust of its speed,
Even as thou, O giant, whom trailed in the wake
of her conquests
Night's sweet despot draws, bound to her ivory
car ;
Man with inviolate caverns, impregnable holds in
his nature,
Depths no storm can pierce, pierced with a shaft
of the sun :
Man that is galled with his confines, and burdened
yet more with his vastness,
Born too great for his ends, never at peace with
his goal ;
Man whom Fate, his victor, magnanimous, clement
in triumph,
Holds as a captive king, mewed in a palace
divine :

Wide its leagues of pleasance, and ample of purview
  its windows;
  Airily falls, in its courts, laughter of fountains
    at play;
Nought, when the harpers are harping, untimely
  reminds him of durance;
  None, as he sits at the feast, whisper Captivity's
    name;
But, would he parley with Silence, withdraw for
  awhile unattended,
  Forth to the beckoning world 'scape for an hour
    and be free,
Lo, his adventurous fancy coercing at once and
  provoking,
  Rise the unscalable walls, built with a word at
    the prime;
Lo, immobile as statues, with pitiless faces of
  iron,
  Armed at each obstinate gate, stand the im-
    passable guards.

III

Miser whose coffered recesses the spoils of eternity
    cumber,
    Spendthrift foaming thy soul wildly in fury
        away,—
We, self-amorous mortals, our own multitudinous
    image
    Seeking in all we behold, seek it and find it in
        thee:
Seek it and find it when o'er us the exquisite fabric
    of Silence
    Perilous-turreted hangs, trembles and dulcetly
        falls;
When the aërial armies engage amid orgies of music,
    Braying of arrogant brass, whimper of querulous
        reeds;
When, at his banquet, the Summer is purple and
    drowsed with repletion;
    When, to his anchorite board, taciturn Winter
        repairs;

When by the tempest are scattered magnificent
    ashes of Autumn ;

When, upon orchard and lane, breaks the white
    foam of the Spring :

When, in extravagant revel, the Dawn, a bacchante
    upleaping,

  Spills, on the tresses of Night, vintages golden
    and red ;

When, as a token at parting, munificent Day, for
    remembrance,

  Gives, unto men that forget, Ophirs of fabulous
    ore ;

When, invincibly rushing, in luminous palpitant
    deluge,

  Hot from the summits of Life, poured is the lava
    of noon ;

When, as yonder, thy mistress, at height of her
    mutable glories,

  Wise from the magical East, comes like a sorceress
    pale.

Ah, she comes, she arises,—impassive, emotionless,
    bloodless,

Wasted and ashen of cheek, zoning her ruins with
pearl.
Once she was warm, she was joyous, desire in her
pulses abounding :
Surely thou lovedst her well, then, in her conquering youth !
Surely not all unimpassioned, at sound of thy rough
serenading,
She, from the balconied night, unto her melodist
leaned,—
Leaned unto thee, her bondsman, who keepest
to-day her commandments,
All for the sake of old love, dead at thy heart
though it lie.

IV

Yea, it is we, light perverts, that waver, and shift
our allegiance ;
We, whom insurgence of blood dooms to be barren
and waste ;

We, unto Nature imputing our frailties, our fever
and tumult ;
  We, that with dust of our strife sully the hue of
her peace.

Thou, with punctual service, fulfillest thy task, being
constant ;
  Thine but to ponder the Law, labour and greatly
obey :

Wherefore, with leapings of spirit, thou chantest
the chant of the faithful,
  Chantest aloud at thy toil, cleansing the Earth of
her stain ;

Leagued in antiphonal chorus with stars and the
populous Systems,
  Following these as their feet dance to the rhyme
of the Suns ;

Thou thyself but a billow, a ripple, a drop of that Ocean,
  Which, labyrinthine of arm, folding us meshed
in its coil,

Shall, as now, with elations, august exultations and
ardours,
  Pour, in unfaltering tide, all its unanimous waves,

HYMN TO THE SEA

When, from this threshold of being, these steps of
    the Presence, this precinct,
Into the matrix of Life darkly divinely resumed,
Man and his littleness perish, erased like an error
    and cancelled,
Man and his greatness survive, lost in the great-
    ness of God.

EPIGRAM

IN mid whirl of the dance of Time ye start,
    Start at the cold touch of Eternity,
And cast your cloaks about you, and depart.—
    The minstrels pause not in their minstrelsy.

FRANCE

25TH JUNE 1894*

LIGHT-HEARTED heroine of tragic story !
Nation whom storm on storm of ruining fate
Unruined leaves,—nay, fairer, more elate,
Hungrier for action, more athirst for glory !
World-witching queen, from fiery floods and gory
Rising eternally regenerate,
Clothed with great deeds and crowned with dreams
            more great
Spacious as Fancy's boundless territory !

Little thou lov'st our island, and perchance
Thou heed'st as little her reluctant praise ;
Yet let her, in these dark and bodeful days,
Sinking old hatreds 'neath the sundering brine,
Immortal and indomitable France,
Marry her tears, her alien tears, to thine.

* The day after the murder of Carnot.

184

A RIDDLE OF THE THAMES

AT windows that from Westminster
   Look southward to the Lollard's Tower,
She sat, my lovely friend.   A blur
   Of gilded mist,—('twas morn's first hour,)—
Made vague the world : and in the gleam
Shivered the half-awakened stream.

Through tinted vapour looming large,
   Ambiguous shapes obscurely rode.
She gazed where many a laden barge
   Like some dim-moving saurian showed.
And 'midst them, lo ! two swans appeared,
And proudly up the river steered.

185

A RIDDLE OF THE THAMES

Two stately swans! What did they there?
   Whence came they? Whither would they go?
Think of them,—things so faultless fair,—
   'Mid the black shipping down below!
On through the rose and gold they passed,
And melted in the morn at last.

Ah, can it be, that they had come,
   Where Thames in sullied glory flows,
Fugitive rebels, tired of some
   Secluded lake's ornate repose,
Eager to taste the life that pours
Its muddier wave 'twixt mightier shores?

We ne'er shall know: our wonderment
   No barren certitude shall mar.
They left behind them, as they went,
   A dream than knowledge ampler far;
And from our world they sailed away
Into some visionary day.

THE YEAR'S MINSTRELSY

SPRING, the low prelude of a lordlier song :
   Summer, a music without hint of death :
Autumn, a cadence lingeringly long :
   Winter, a pause ;—the Minstrel-Year takes breath.

A STUDY IN CONTRASTS

I

BY cliff and chine, and hollow-nestling wood
Thrilled with the poignant savour of the sea,
All in the crisp light of a wintry morn,
We walked, my friend and I, preceded still
By one whose silken and voluminous suit,
His courtly ruff, snow-pure 'mid golden tan,
His grandly feathered legs slenderly strong,
The broad and flowing billow of his breast,
His delicate ears and superfine long nose,
With that last triumph, his distinguished tail,
In their collective glory spoke his race
The flower of Collie aristocracy.
Yet, from his traits, how absent that reserve,

A STUDY IN CONTRASTS

That stillness on a base of power, which marks,

In men and mastiffs, the selectly sprung!

For after all, his high-life attributes,

His trick of doing nothing with an air,

His *salon* manners and society smile,

Were but skin-deep, factitious, and you saw

The bustling despot of the mountain flock,

And pastoral dog-of-all-work, underlie

The fashionable modern lady's pet,—

Industrial impulses bereft of scope,

Duty and discipline denied an aim,

Ancestral energy and strenuousness

In graceful trifling frittered all away.

Witness the depth of his concern and zeal

About minutest issues: shall we take

This path or that?—it matters not a straw—

But just a moment unresolved we stand,

And all his personality, from ears

To tip of tail, is interrogative;

And when from pure indifference we decide,

How he vociferates! how he bounds ahead!

With what enthusiasm he ratifies,

A STUDY IN CONTRASTS

Applauds, acclaims our choice 'twixt right and left,
As though some hoary problem over which
The world had puckered immemorial brows,
Were solved at last, and all life launched anew!

These and a thousand tricks and ways and traits
I noted as of Demos at their root,
And foreign to the staid, conservative,
Came-over-with-the-Conqueror type of mind.
And then, his nature, how impressionable,
How quickly moved to Collie mirth or woe,
Elated or dejected at a word!
And how unlike your genuine Vere de Vere's
Frigid, indifferent, half-ignoring glance
At everything outside the sacred pale
Of things De Veres have sanctioned from the
        Flood,
The unweariable curiosity
And universal open-mindedness
Of that all-testing, all-inquisitive nose!

A STUDY IN CONTRASTS

II

So, to my friend's house, back we strolled; and
    there—
We loitering in the garden—from her post
Of purview at a window, languidly
A great Angora watched his Collieship,
And throned in monumental calm, surveyed
His effervescence, volatility,
Clamour on slight occasion, fussiness,
Herself immobile, imperturbable,
Like one whose vision seeks the Immanent
Behind these symbols and appearances,
The face within this transitory mask.
And as her eyes with indolent regard
Viewed his upbubblings of ebullient life,
She seemed the Orient Spirit incarnate, lost
In contemplation of the Western Soul!
Ev'n so, methought, the genius of the East,
Reposeful, patient, undemonstrative,
Luxurious, enigmatically sage,

A STUDY IN CONTRASTS

Dispassionately cruel, might look down
On all the fever of the Occident ;—
The brooding mother of the unfilial world,
Recumbent on her own antiquity,
Aloof from our mutations and unrest,
Alien to our achievements and desires,
Too proud alike for protest or assent
When new thoughts thunder at her massy door ;—
Another brain dreaming another dream,
Another heart recalling other loves,
Too grey and grave for our adventurous hopes,
For our precipitate pleasures too august,
And in majestic taciturnity
Refraining her illimitable scorn.

TO RICHARD HOLT HUTTON

YES, I have had my griefs; and yet
I think that when I shake off life's annoy,
    I shall, in my last hour, forget
        All things that were not joy.

Have I not watched the starry throngs
Dance, and the soul of April break in bud?
    Have I not taken Schubert's songs
        Into my brain and blood?

I have seen the morn one laugh of gold;
I have known a mind that was a match for Fate;
    I have wondered what the heavens can hold
        Than simplest love more great.

TO RICHARD HOLT HUTTON

And not uncrowned with honours ran

My days, and not without a boast shall end !

For I was Shakespeare's countryman ;

And wert thou not my friend ?

THE beasts in field are glad, and have not wit
  To know why leapt their hearts when springtime
     shone.
Man looks at his own bliss, considers it,
  Weighs it with curious fingers : and 'tis gone.

DOMINE, QUO VADIS?

A Legend of the Early Church

DARKENING the azure roof of Nero's world,
From smouldering Rome the smoke of ruin curled;
And the fierce populace went clamouring—
"These Christian dogs, 'tis they have done this thing!"
So to the wild wolf Hate were sacrificed
The panting, huddled flock whose crime was Christ.

   Now Peter lodged in Rome, and rose each morn
Looking to be ere night in sunder torn
By those blind hands that with inebriate zeal
Burned the strong Saints, or broke them on the
      wheel,
Or flung them to the lions to make mirth
For dames that ruled the lords that ruled the earth.

DOMINE, QUO VADIS?

And unto him, their towering rocky hold,
Repaired those sheep of the Good Shepherd's fold
In whose white fleece as yet no blood or foam
Bare witness to the ravening fangs of Rome.
" More light, more cheap," they cried, " we hold our
    lives
Than chaff the flail or dust the whirlwind drives :
As chaff they are winnowed and as dust are blown ;
Nay, they are nought ; but priceless is thine own.
Not in yon streaming shambles must thou die :
We counsel, we entreat, we charge thee, fly !"
And Peter answered : " Nay, my place is here ;
Through the dread storm, this ship of Christ I steer.
Blind is the tempest, deaf the roaring tide,
And I, His pilot, at the helm abide."

Then one stood forth, the flashing of whose soul
Enrayed his presence like an aureole.
Eager he spake ; his fellows, ere they heard,
Caught from his eyes the swift and leaping word.
" Let *us*, His vines, be in the wine-press trod,
And poured a beverage for the lips of God :

Or, ground as wheat of His eternal field,
Bread for His table let our bodies yield.
Behold, the Church hath other use for thee
Thy safety is her own, and thou must flee.
Ours be the glory at her call to die,
But quick and whole God needs His great ally."
And Peter said : "Do lords of spear and shield
Thus leave their hosts uncaptained on the field,
And from some mount of prospect watch afar
The havoc of the hurricane of war?
Yet, if He wills it. . . . Nay, my task is plain, —
To serve, and to endure, and to remain.
But weak I stand, and I beseech you all
Urge me no more, lest at a touch I fall."

There knelt a noble youth at Peter's feet,
And like a viol's strings his voice was sweet.
A suppliant angel might have pleaded so,
Crowned with the splendour of some starry woe.
He said : "My sire and brethren yesterday
The heathen did with ghastly torments slay.

DOMINE, QUO VADIS?

Pain, like a worm, beneath their feet they trod.

Their souls went up like incense unto God.

An offering richer yet, can Heaven require?

O live, and be my brethren and my sire."

And Peter answered: "Son, there is small need

That thou exhort me to the easier deed.

Rather I would that thou and these had lent

Strength to uphold, not shatter, my intent.

Already my resolve is shaken sore.

I pray thee, if thou love me, say no more."

And even as he spake, he went apart,

Somewhat to hide the brimming of his heart,

Wherein a voice came flitting to and fro,

That now said "Tarry!" and anon said "Go!"

And louder every moment, "Go!" it cried,

And "Tarry!" to a whisper sank, and died.

And as a leaf when summer is o'erpast

Hangs trembling ere it fall in some chance blast,

So hung his trembling purpose and fell dead;

And he arose, and hurried forth, and fled,

DOMINE, QUO VADIS?

Darkness conniving, through the Capuan Gate,
From all that heaven of love, that hell of hate,
To the Campania glimmering wide and still,
And strove to think he did his Master's will.

But spectral eyes and mocking tongues pursued,
And with vague hands he fought a phantom
brood.
Doubts, like a swarm of gnats, o'erhung his flight,
And " Lord," he prayed, " have I not done aright ?
Can I not, living, more avail for Thee
Than whelmed in you red storm of agony ?
The tempest, it shall pass, and I remain,
Not from its fiery sickle saved in vain.
Are there no seeds to sow, no desert lands
Waiting the tillage of these eager hands,
That I should beastlike 'neath the butcher fall,
More fruitlessly than oxen from the stall ?
Is earth so easeful, is men's hate so sweet,
Are thorns so welcome unto sleepless feet,
Have death and heaven so feeble lures, that I,
Choosing to live, should win rebuke thereby ?

DOMINE, QUO VADIS?

Not mine the dread of pain, the lust of bliss!
Master who judgest, have I done amiss?"

Lo, on the darkness brake a wandering ray :
A vision flashed along the Appian Way.
Divinely in the pagan night it shone—
A mournful Face—a Figure hurrying on—
Though haggard and dishevelled, frail and worn,
A King, of David's lineage, crowned with thorn.
"Lord, whither farest?" Peter, wondering, cried.
"To Rome," said Christ, "to be re-crucified."

Into the night the vision ebbed like breath ;
And Peter turned, and rushed on Rome and
  death.

TO AUBREY DE VERE

POET, whose grave and strenuous lyre is still
For Truth and Duty strung: whose art eschews
The lighter graces of the softer Muse,
Disdainful of mere craftsman's idle skill:
Yours is a soul from visionary hill
Watching and hearkening for ethereal news,
Looking beyond life's storms and death's cold dews
To habitations of the eternal will.

Not mine your mystic creed; not mine, in prayer
And worship, at the ensanguined Cross to kneel;
But when I mark your faith how pure and fair,
How based on love, on passion for man's weal,
My mind, half envying what it cannot share,
Reveres the reverence which it cannot feel.

CHRISTMAS DAY

THE morn broke bright : the thronging people wore
Their best : but in the general face I saw
No touch of veneration or of awe.
Christ's natal day ? 'Twas merely one day more
On which the mart agreed to close its door ;
A lounging-time by usage and by law
Sanctioned ; nor recked they, beyond this, one straw
Of any meaning which for man it bore !

Fated among time's fallen leaves to stray,
We breathe an air that savours of the tomb,
Heavy with dissolution and decay ;
Waiting till some new world-emotion rise,
And with the shattering might of the simoom
Sweep clean this dying Past that never dies.

TO A LADY RECOVERED FROM A DANGEROUS SICKNESS

LIFE plucks thee back as by the golden hair—
  Life, who had feigned to let thee go but now.
Wealthy is Death already, and can spare
  Ev'n such a prey as thou.

A NEW NATIONAL ANTHEM

GOD save our ancient land,
God bless our noble land,
   God save this land !
Yea, from war's pangs and fears,
Plague's tooth and famine's tears,
Ev'n unto latest years
   God save this land !

God bless our reigning race !
Truth, honour, wisdom, grace,
   Guide their right hand !
Yet, though we love their sway,
England is more than they :
God bless their realm, we pray,
   God save our land !

Too long the gulf betwixt
This man and that man fixt
    Yawns yet unspanned.
Too long, that some may rest,
Tired millions toil unblest.
God lift our lowliest,
    God save this land !

God save our ancient land,
God bless our noble land,
    God save our land !
Earth's empires wax and wane,
Man's might is mown as grain :
God's arm our arm sustain !
    God save our land !

TO Art we go as to a well, athirst,
  And see our shadow 'gainst its mimic skies,
But in its depth must plunge and be immersed
  To clasp the naiad Truth where low she lies.

SONNET

I THINK the immortal servants of mankind,
Who, from their graves, watch by how slow degrees
The World-Soul greatens with the centuries,
Mourn most Man's barren levity of mind,
The ear to no grave harmonies inclined,
The witless thirst for false wit's worthless lees,
The laugh mistimed in tragic presences,
The eye to all majestic meanings blind.

O prophets, martyrs, saviours, *ye* were great,
All truth being great to you : ye deemed Man more
Than a dull jest, God's ennui to amuse :
The world, for you, held purport : Life ye wore
Proudly, as Kings their solemn robes of state ;
And humbly, as the mightiest monarchs use.

208

I DO not ask to have my fill
    Of wine, or love, or fame.
I do not, for a little ill,
    Against the gods exclaim.

One boon of Fortune I implore,
    With one petition kneel:
At least caress me not, before
    Thou break me on thy wheel.

ODE IN MAY

L<small>ET</small> me go forth, and share
The overflowing Sun
With one wise friend, or one
Better than wise, being fair,
Where the pewit wheels and dips
On heights of bracken and ling,
And Earth, unto her leaflet tips,
Tingles with the Spring.

What is so sweet and dear
As a prosperous morn in May,
The confident prime of the day,
And the dauntless youth of the year,
210

ODE IN MAY

When nothing that asks for bliss,
Asking aright, is denied,
And half of the world a bridegroom is,
And half of the world a bride?

The Song of Mingling flows,
Grave, ceremonial, pure,
As once, from lips that endure,
The cosmic descant rose,
When the temporal lord of life,
Going his golden way,
Had taken a wondrous maid to wife
That long had said him nay.

For of old the Sun, our sire,
Came wooing the mother of men,
Earth, that was virginal then,
Vestal fire to his fire.
Silent her bosom and coy,
But the strong god sued and pressed;
And born of their starry nuptial joy
Are all that drink of her breast.

211

And the triumph of him that begot,

And the travail of her that bore,

Behold, they are evermore

As warp and weft in our lot.

We are children of splendour and fame,

Of shuddering, also, and tears.

Magnificent out of the dust we came,

And abject from the Spheres.

O bright irresistible lord,

We are fruit of Earth's womb, each one,

And fruit of thy loins, O Sun,

Whence first was the seed outpoured.

To thee as our Father we bow,

Forbidden thy Father to see,

Who is older and greater than thou, as thou

Art greater and older than we.

Thou art but as a word of his speech,

Thou art but as a wave of his hand;

Thou art brief as a glitter of sand

'Twixt tide and tide on his beach;

ODE IN MAY

Thou art less than a spark of his fire,

Or a moment's mood of his soul:

Thou art lost in the notes on the lips
    of his choir

That chant the chant of the Whole.

SONG

OH, like a queen's her happy tread,
And like a queen's her golden head!
But oh, at last, when all is said,
  Her woman's heart for me!

We wandered where the river gleamed
'Neath oaks that mused and pines that dreamed.
A wild thing of the woods she seemed,
  So proud, and pure, and free!

All heaven drew nigh to hear her sing,
When from her lips her soul took wing:
The oaks forgot their pondering,
  The pines their reverie.
214

SONG

And oh, her happy queenly tread,
And oh, her queenly golden head!
But oh, her heart, when all is said,
Her woman's heart for me!

THE WORLD IN ARMOUR

I

UNDER this shade of crimson wings abhorred
That never wholly leaves the sky serene,—
While Vengeance sleeps a sleep so light, between
Dominions that acclaim Thee overlord,—
Sadly the blast of Thy tremendous word,
Whate'er its mystic purport may have been.
Echoes across the ages, Nazarene :
Not to bring peace Mine errand, but a sword.

For lo, Thy world uprises and lies down
In armour, and its Peace is War, in all
Save the great death that weaves War's dreadful
    crown ;
War unennobled by heroic pain,
War where none triumph, none sublimely fall,
War that sits smiling, with the eyes of Cain.

THE WORLD IN ARMOUR

II

When London's Plague, that day by day enrolled
His thousands dead, nor deigned his rage to abate
Till grass was green in silent Bishopsgate,
Had come and passed like thunder,—still, 'tis told,
The monster, driven to earth, in hovels old
And haunts obscure, though dormant, lingered late,
Till the dread Fire, one roaring wave of fate,
Rose, and swept clean his last retreat and hold.

In Europe live the dregs of Plague to-day,
Dregs of full many an ancient Plague and dire,
Old wrongs, old lies of ages blind and cruel,
What if alone the world-war's world-wide fire
Can purge the ambushed pestilence away?
Yet woe to him that idly lights the fuel!

III

A moment's fantasy, the vision came
Of Europe dipped in fiery death, and so
Mounting re-born, with vestal limbs aglow,
Splendid and fragrant from her bath of flame.
It fleeted; and a phantom without name,
Sightless, dismembered, terrible, said : "Lo,
I am that ravished Europe men shall know
After the morn of blood and night of shame."

The spectre passed, and I beheld alone
The Europe of the present, as she stands,
Powerless from terror of her own vast power,
Neath novel stars, beside a brink unknown ;
And round her the sad Kings, with sleepless hands,
Piling the fagots, hour by doomful hour.

TO A FRIEND

Uniting Antiquarian Tastes with Progressive Politics

TRUE lover of the Past, who dost not scorn
To give good heed to what the Future saith,—
Drinking the air of two worlds at a breath,
Thou livest not alone in thoughts outworn,
But ever helpest the new time be born,
Though with a sigh for the old order's death ;
As clouds that crown the night that perisheth
Aid in the high solemnities of morn.

Guests of the ages, at To-morrow's door
Why shrink we ?   The long track behind us lies,
The lamps gleam and the music throbs before,
Bidding us enter: and I count him wise,
Who loves so well Man's noble memories
He needs must love Man's nobler hopes yet more.

AN EPITAPH

HIS friends he loved.   His fellest earthly foes—
  Cats—I believe he did but feign to hate.
My hand will miss the insinuated nose,
    Mine eyes the tail that wagg'd contempt at
      Fate.

PEACE AND WAR

THE sleek sea, gorged and sated, basking lies;
The cruel creature fawns and blinks and purrs;
And almost we forget what fangs are hers,
And trust for once her emerald-golden eyes;
Though haply on the morrow she shall rise
And summon her infernal ministers,
And charge her everlasting barriers,
With wild white fingers snatching at the skies.

So, betwixt Peace and War, man's life is cast;
Yet hath he dreamed of perfect Peace at last
Shepherding all the nations ev'n as sheep.
The inconstant, moody ocean shall as soon,
At the cold dictates of the bloodless moon,
Swear an eternity of halcyon sleep.

TO ——

FORGET not, brother singer! that though Prose
  Can never be too truthful or too wise,
Song is not Truth, not Wisdom, but the rose
  Upon Truth's lips, the light in Wisdom's eyes.

222

SONG IN IMITATION OF THE ELIZABETHANS

SWEETEST sweets that time hath rifled,
   Live anew on lyric tongue—
Tresses with which Paris trifled,
   Lips to Antony's that clung.
These surrender not their rose,
Nor their golden puissance those.

Vain the envious loam that covers
   Her of Egypt, her of Troy :
Helen's, Cleopatra's lovers
   Still desire them, still enjoy.
Fate but stole what Song restored :
Vain the aspic, vain the cord.

Idly clanged the sullen portal,
  Idly the sepulchral door :
Fame the mighty, Love the immortal,
  These than foolish dust are more :
Nor may captive Death refuse
Homage to the conquering Muse.

EPIGRAM

FOR metaphors of man we search the skies,
    And find our allegory in all the air.
We gaze on Nature with Narcissus-eyes,
    Enamour'd of our shadow everywhere.

THE FRONTIER

AT the hushed brink of twilight,—when, as though
Some solemn journeying phantom paused to lay
An ominous finger on the awestruck day,
Earth holds her breath till that great presence go,—
A moment comes of visionary glow,
Pendulous 'twixt the gold hour and the grey,
Lovelier than these, more eloquent than they
Of memory, foresight, and life's ebb and flow.

So have I known, in some fair woman's face,
While viewless yet was Time's more gross imprint,
The first, faint, hesitant, elusive hint
Of that invasion of the vandal years
Seem deeper beauty than youth's cloudless grace,
Wake subtler dreams, and touch me nigh to tears.

THE LURE

COME hither and behold them, Sweet—
　　The fairy prow that o'er me rides,
And white sails of a lagging Fleet
　　On idle tides.

Come hither and behold them, Sweet—
　　The lustrous gloom, the vivid shade,
The throats of love that burn and beat
　　And shake the glade.

Come, for the hearts of all things pine,
　　And all the paths desire thy feet,
And all this beauty asks for thine,
　　As I do, Sweet!

EPIGRAM

LOVE, like a bird, hath perch'd upon a spray
   For thee and me to hearken what he sings.
Contented, he forgets to fly away ;
   But hush ! . . . remind not Eros of his wings.

THE PROTEST

BID me no more to other eyes
  With wandering worship fare,
And weave my numbers garland-wise
  To crown another's hair.
On me no more a mandate lay
Thou wouldst not have me to obey!

Bid me no more to leave unkissed
  That rose-wreathed porch of pearl.
Shall I, where'er the winds may list,
  Give them my life to whirl?
Perchance too late thou wilt be fain
Thy exile to recall—in vain.

THE PROTEST

Bid me no more from thee depart,
   For in thy voice to-day
I hear the tremor of thy heart
   Entreating me to stay ;
I hear . . . nay, silence tells it best,
O yielded lips, O captive breast !

SINCE Life is rough,
  Sing smoothly, O Bard.
Enough, enough,
  To have *found* Life hard !

No record Art keeps
  Of her travail and throes.
There is toil on the steeps ;
  On the summits, repose.

THE TOMB OF BURNS

WHAT woos the world to yonder shrine?
What sacred clay, what dust divine?
Was this some Master faultless-fine,
    In whom we praise
The cunning of the jewelled line
    And carven phrase?

A searcher of our source and goal,
A reader of God's secret scroll?
A Shakespeare, flashing o'er the whole
    Of man's domain
The splendour of his cloudless soul
    And perfect brain?

THE TOMB OF BURNS

Some Keats, to Grecian gods allied,
Clasping all Beauty as his bride?
Some Shelley, soaring dim-descried
    Above Time's throng,
And heavenward hurling wild and wide
    His spear of song?

A lonely Wordsworth, from the crowd
Half hid in light, half veiled in cloud?
A sphere-born Milton cold and proud,
    In hallowing dews
Dipt, and with gorgeous ritual vowed
    Unto the Muse?

Nay, none of these,—and little skilled
On heavenly heights to sing and build!
Thine, thine, O Earth, whose fields he tilled,
    And thine alone,
Was he whose fiery heart lies stilled
    'Neath yonder stone.

THE TOMB OF BURNS

He came when poets had forgot
How rich and strange the human lot;
How warm the tints of Life; how hot
        Are Love and Hate;
And what makes Truth divine, and what
        Makes Manhood great.

A ghostly troop, in pale amaze
They melted 'neath that living gaze,—
His in whose spirit's gusty blaze
        We seem to hear
The crackling of their phantom bays
        Sapless and sear!

For, 'mid an age of dust and dearth,
Once more had bloomed immortal worth.
There, in the strong, splenetic North,
        The Spring began.
A mighty mother had brought forth
        A mighty man.

THE TOMB OF BURNS

No mystic torch through Time he bore,
No virgin veil from Life he tore;
His soul no bright insignia wore
    Of starry birth;
He saw what all men see—no more—
    In heaven and earth:

But as, when thunder crashes nigh,
All darkness opes one flaming eye,
And the world leaps against the sky,—
    So fiery-clear
Did the old truths that we pass by
    To him appear.

How could he 'scape the doom of such
As feel the airiest phantom-touch
Keenlier than others feel the clutch
    Of iron powers,—
Who die of having lived so much
    In their large hours?

THE TOMB OF BURNS

He erred, he sinned: and if there be
Who, from his hapless frailties free,
Rich in the poorer virtues, see
    His faults alone,—
To such, O Lord of Charity,
    Be mercy shown!

Singly he faced the bigot brood,
The meanly wise, the feebly good;
He pelted them with pearl, with mud;
    He fought them well,—
But ah, the stupid million stood,
    And he—he fell!

All bright and glorious at the start,
'Twas his ignobly to depart,
Slain by his own too affluent heart,
    Too generous blood;
And blindly, having lost Life's chart,
    To meet Death's flood.

THE TOMB OF BURNS

So closes the fantastic fray,
The duel of the spirit and clay !
So come bewildering disarray
  And blurring gloom,
The irremediable day
  And final doom.

So passes, all confusedly
As lights that hurry, shapes that flee
About some brink we dimly see,
  The trivial, great,
Squalid, majestic tragedy
  Of human fate.

Not ours to gauge the more or less,
The will's defect, the blood's excess,
The earthy humours that oppress
  The radiant mind.
His greatness, not his littleness,
  Concerns mankind.

THE TOMB OF BURNS

A dreamer of the common dreams,
A fisher in familiar streams,
He chased the transitory gleams
  That all pursue ;
But on his lips the eternal themes
  Again were new.

With shattering ire or withering mirth
He smote each worthless claim to worth.
The barren fig-tree cumbering Earth
  He would not spare.
Through ancient lies of proudest birth
  He drove his share.

To him the Powers that formed him brave,
Yet weak to breast the fatal wave,
A mighty gift of Hatred gave,—
  A gift above
All other gifts benefic, save
  The gift of Love.

THE TOMB OF BURNS

He saw 'tis meet that Man possess
The will to curse as well as bless,
To pity—and be pitiless,
　　　To make, and mar ;
The fierceness that from tenderness
　　　Is never far.

And so his fierce and tender strain
Lives, and his idlest words remain
To flout oblivion, that in vain
　　　Strives to destroy
One lightest record of his pain
　　　Or of his joy.

And though thrice statelier names decay,
His own can wither not away
While plighted lass and lad shall stray
　　　Among the broom,
Where evening touches glen and brae
　　　With rosy gloom ;

THE TOMB OF BURNS

While Hope and Love with Youth abide ;
While Age sits at the ingleside ;
While yet there have not wholly died
          The heroic fires,
The patriot passion, and the pride
          In noble sires ;

While, with the conquering Teuton breed
Whose fair estate of speech and deed
Heritors north and south of Tweed
          Alike may claim,
The dimly mingled Celtic seed
          Flowers like a flame ;

While nations see in holy trance
That vision of the world's advance
Which glorified his countenance
          When from afar
He hailed the Hope that shot o'er France
          Its crimson star ;

240

While, plumed for flight, the Soul deplores
The cage that foils the wing that soars;
And while, through adamantine doors

    In dreams flung wide,

We hear resound, on mortal shores,

    The immortal tide.

I FOLLOW Beauty; of her train am I :
    Beauty whose voice is earth and sea and air ;
Who serveth, and her hands for all things ply ;
    Who reigneth, and her throne is everywhere.

SONNETS, Etc.,

FROM

"THE YEAR OF SHAME"

Three of the following sonnets appeared also in the Author's pamphlet, "The Purple East."

FROM "THE YEAR OF SHAME"

TO A LADY

DAUGHTER of Ireland,—nay, 'twere better said,
Daughter of Ireland's beauty, Ireland's grace,
Child of her charm, of her romance ; whose face
Is legendary with her glories fled !
The shadow of her living griefs and dead
I pray you to put by a little space,
And mourn with me an ancient Orient race
Outcast and doomed and disinherited.

Though Wrong be strong, though thrones be built
    on crimes,
To know you, Lady, is to doubt no more
That in the world are mightier powers than these ;
That heaven, the ocean, gains on earth, the shore ;
And that deformity and hate are Time's,
And love and loveliness Eternity's.

FROM "THE YEAR OF SHAME"

THE TIRED LION

SPEAK once again, with that great note of
    thine,
Hero withdrawn from Senates and their sound
Unto thy home by Cambria's northern bound,
Not always, not in all things, was it mine
Speak once again, and wake a world supine.
To follow where thou led'st : but who hath found
Another man so shod with fire, so crowned
With thunder, and so armed with wrath divine ?
Lift up thy voice once more ! The nation's heart
Is cold as Anatolia's mountains snows.
Oh, from these alien paths of base repose
Call back thy England, ere thou too depart—
Ere, on some secret mission, thou too start
With silent footsteps, whither no man knows.

THE KNELL OF CHIVALRY

O VANISHED morn of crimson and of gold,
O youth of roselight and romance, wherein
I read of paynim and of paladin,
And Beauty snatched from ogre's dungeoned
    hold !
Ever the recreant would in dust be rolled,
Ever the true knight in the joust would win,
Ever the scaly shape of monstrous Sin
At last lie vanquished, fold on writhing fold.
Was it all false, that world of princely deeds,
The splendid quest, the good fight ringing clear?
Yonder the Dragon ramps with fiery gorge,
Yonder the victim faints and gasps and bleeds ;
But in his merry England our St. George
Sleeps a base sleep beside his idle spear.

FROM "THE YEAR OF SHAME"

A TRIAL OF ORTHODOXY

THE clinging children at their mother's knee
Slain; and the sire and kindred one by one
Flayed or hewn piecemeal; and things nameless
    done,
Not to be told: while imperturbably
The nations gaze, where Neva to the sea,
Where Seine and Rhine, Tiber and Danube run,
And where great armies glitter in the sun,
And great kings rule, and man is boasted free !
What wonder if yon torn and naked throng
Should doubt a Heaven that seems to wink and nod,
And having moaned at noontide, " Lord, how long ? "
Should cry, " Where hidest Thou ? " at evenfall,
At midnight, " Is He deaf and blind, our God ? "
And ere day dawn, " Is He indeed at all ? "

FROM "THE YEAR OF SHAME"

TO THE SULTAN

CALIPH, I did thee wrong.   I hailed thee late
"Abdul the Damned," and would recall my word.
It merged thee with the unillustrious herd
Who crowd the approaches to the infernal gate—
Spirits gregarious, equal in their state
As is the innumerable ocean bird,
Gannet or gull, whose wandering plaint is heard
On Ailsa or Iona desolate.
For, in a world where cruel deeds abound,
The merely damned are legion : with such souls
Is not each hollow and cranny of Tophet
        crammed ?
Thou with the brightest of Hell's aureoles
Dost shine supreme, incomparably crowned,
Immortally, beyond all mortals, damned.

FROM "THE YEAR OF SHAME"

ON THE REPORTED EXPULSION FROM FRANCE OF AHMED RIZA,

A Disaffected Subject of the Sultan

WHEN, from supreme disaster, France uprose,
Shook her great wings and faced the world anew,
Who, if not we, rejoiced at heart to view
Her proud resilience after mightiest woes?
When 'neath the anarch's knife we saw the close
Of Carnot's day, amid her weepings who
Wept if not we, for the just man and true
That masked his strength in most urbane repose?
And now again we mourn, but not with her,
Nay, not with her, though for her!—mourn to see
A tyrant, Hell's most perfect minister,
A man-fiend, sun him in her countenance;
And Freedom, whose impassioned name was France,
  Lie soiled and desecrate by France the Free.

FROM "THE YEAR OF SHAME"

ON A CERTAIN EUROPEAN ALLIANCE

THE Hercules of nations, shaggy-browed,
Enormous-limbed, supreme on Steppe and plain
Dwelt without consort, in his narrow brain
Nursing wide dreams he might not dream aloud;
Till him the radiant western Venus vowed
(So strange is love!) she pined for: and these twain
Were wedded—Neptune, with his nereid-train,
Gracing the pageant of their nuptials proud.

Perfect in amorous arts, through eyes and ears
She fans her giant's not too fierce desire.
"How long, O Venus? What impassioned years,
What ages of such rapture, ere thou tire?"
Thus the lewd gods: thus Mars and all his peers,
Gazing profane, at fault 'twixt mirth and ire.

FROM "THE YEAR OF SHAME"

TO OUR SOVEREIGN LADY

QUEEN, that from Spring to Autumn of Thy reign
Hast taught Thy people how 'tis queenlier far
Than any golden pomp of peace or war,
Simply to be a woman without stain!
Queen whom we love, Who lovest us again!
We pray that yonder, by Thy wild Braemar,
The lord of many legions, the White Czar,
At this red hour, hath tarried not in vain.
We dream that from Thy words, perhaps Thy
        tears,
Ev'n in the King's inscrutable heart, shall grow
Harvest of succour, weal, and gentler days!
So shall Thy lofty name to latest years
Still loftier sound, and ever sweetlier blow
The rose of Thy imperishable praise.

FROM "THE YEAR OF SHAME"

EUROPE AT THE PLAY

O LANGUID audience, met to see
The last act of the tragedy
On that terrific stage afar,
Where burning towns the footlights are,—
O listless Europe, day by day
Callously sitting out the play!

So sat, with loveless count'nance cold,
Round the arena, Rome of old.
Pain, and the ebb of life's red tide,
So, with a calm regard, she eyed,
Her gorgeous vesture, million-pearled,
Splashed with the blood of half the world.
High was her glory's noon: as yet
She had not dreamed her sun could set!

FROM "THE YEAR OF SHAME"

As yet she had not dreamed how soon
Shadows should vex her glory's noon.
Another's pangs she counted nought;
Of human hearts she took no thought;
But God, at nightfall, in her ear
Thundered *His* thought exceeding clear.

Perchance in tempest and in blight,
On Europe, too, shall fall the night!
She sees the victim overborne,
By worse than ravening lions torn.
She sees, she hears, with soul unstirred,
And lifts no hand, and speaks no word,
But vaunts a brow like theirs who deem
Men's wrongs a phrase, men's rights a dream.
Yet haply she shall learn, too late,
In some blind hurricane of Fate,
How fierily alive the things
She held as fool's imaginings,
And, though circuitous and obscure,
The feet of Nemesis how sure.

ESTRANGEMENT

SO, without overt breach, we fall apart,
Tacitly sunder—neither you nor I
Conscious of one intelligible Why,
And both, from severance, winning equal smart.
So, with resigned and acquiescent heart,
Whene'er your name on some chance lip may lie,
I seem to see an alien shade pass by,
A spirit wherein I have no lot or part.
Thus may a captive, in some fortress grim,
From casual speech betwixt his warders, learn
That June on her triumphal progress goes
Through arched and bannered woodlands; while for
    him
She is a legend emptied of concern,
And idle is the rumour of the rose.

THE gods man makes he breaks; proclaims them
  each
  Immortal, and himself outlives them all;
But whom he set not up he cannot reach
  To shake His cloud-dark sun-bright pedestal.

THE LOST EDEN

BUT yesterday was Man from Eden driven.
His dream, wherein he dreamed himself the first
Of creatures, fashioned for eternity—
This was the Eden that he shared with Eve.

Eve, the adventurous soul within his soul!
The sleepless, the unslaked! She showed him where
Amidst his pleasance hung the bough whose fruit
Is disenchantment and the perishing
Of many glorious errors. And he saw
His paradise how narrow: and he saw,—
He, who had well-nigh deemed the world itself
Of less significance and majesty
Than his own part and business in it!—how
Little that part, and in how great a world.

THE LOST EDEN

And an imperative world-thirst drave him forth,
And the gold gates of Eden clanged behind.

Never shall he return : for he hath sent
His spirit abroad among the infinitudes,
And may no more to the ancient pales recall
The travelled feet.   But oftentimes he feels
The intolerable vastness bow him down,
The awful homeless spaces scare his soul ;
And half-regretful he remembers then
His Eden lost, as some grey mariner
May think of the far fields where he was bred,
And woody ways unbreathed-on by the sea,
Though more familiar now the ocean-paths
Gleam, and the stars his fathers never knew.

EPIGRAM

ONWARD the chariot of the Untarrying moves;
  Nor day divulges him nor night conceals;
Thou hear'st the echo of unreturning hooves
  And thunder of irrevocable wheels.

INVENTION

I ENVY not the Lark his song divine,
  Nor thee, O Maid, thy beauty's faultless
    mould.
Perhaps the chief felicity is mine,
    Who hearken and behold.

The joy of the Artificer Unknown
  Whose genius could devise the Lark and thee—
This, or a kindred rapture, let me own,
    I covet ceaselessly!

EPIGRAM

I PLUCK'D this flower, O brighter flower, for thee
There where the river dies into the sea.
To kiss it the wild west wind hath made free :
Kiss it thyself and give it back to me.

AN INSCRIPTION AT WINDERMERE

GUEST of this fair abode, before thee rise
No summits vast, that icily remote
Cannot forget their own magnificence
Or once put off their kinghood; but withal
A confraternity of stateliest brows,
As Alp or Atlas noble, in port and mien;
Old majesties, that on their secular seats
Enthroned, are yet of affable access
And easy audience, not too great for praise,
Not arrogantly aloof from thy concerns,
Not vaunting their indifference to thy fate,
Nor so august as to contemn thy love.
Do homage to these suavely eminent;
But privy to their bosoms wouldst thou be,
There is a vale, whose seaward parted lips

Murmur eternally some half-divulged
Reluctant secret, where thou may'st o'erhear
The mountains interchange their confidences,
Peak with his federate peak, that think aloud
Their broad and lucid thoughts, in liberal day :
Thither repair alone : the mountain heart
Not two may enter ; thence returning, tell
What thou hast heard ; and 'mid the immortal
    friends
Of mortals, the selectest fellowship
Of poets divine, place shall be found for thee.

SONG

APRIL, April,
Laugh thy girlish laughter;
Then, the moment after,
Weep thy girlish tears!
April, that mine ears
Like a lover greetest,
If I tell thee, sweetest,
All my hopes and fears,
April, April,
Laugh thy golden laughter,
But, the moment after,
Weep thy golden tears!

All, vain, thrice vain in the end, thy hate and rage,
And the shrill tempest of thy clamorous page.
True poets but transcendent lovers be,
And one great love-confession poesy.

ELUSION

WHERE shall I find thee, Joy? by what great
    marge
With the strong seas exulting? on what peaks
Rapt? or astray within what forest bourn,
Thy light hands parting the resilient boughs?

Hast thou no answer? . . . Ah, in mine own
    breast
Except unsought thou spring, though I go forth
And tease the waves for news of thee, and
    make
Importunate inquisition of the woods
If thou didst pass that way, I shall but find
The brief print of thy footfall on sere leaves
And the salt brink, and woo thy touch in vain.

EPIGRAM

IMMURED in sense, with fivefold bonds confined,
  Rest we content if whispers from the stars
In waftings of the incalculable wind
  Come blown at midnight through our prison-bars.

TOO LATE

TOO late to say farewell,
To turn, and fall asunder, and forget,
And take up the dropped life of yesterday !
So ancient, so far-off, is yesterday,
To the last hour ere I had kissed thy cheek !
Too late to say farewell.

Too late to say farewell.
Can aught remain hereafter as of old ?
A touch, a tone hath changed the heaven and
earth,
And in a hand-clasp all begins anew.
Somewhat of me is thine, of thee is mine.
Too late to say farewell.

TOO LATE

Too late to say farewell.

We are not May-day masquers, thou and I !

We have lived deep life, we have drunk of tragic
springs.

'Tis for light hearts to take light leave of love,

But ah, for me, for thee, too late, dear Spirit !

Too late to say farewell.

THEY AND WE

WITH stormy joy, from height on height,
 The thundering torrents leap.
The mountain tops, with still delight,
 Their great inaction keep.

Man only, irked by calm, and rent,
 By each emotion's throes,
Neither in passion finds content,
 Nor finds it in repose.

EPIGRAM

THINK not thy wisdom can illume away
The ancient tanglement of night and day.
Enough, to acknowledge both, and both revere :
They see not clearliest who see all things clear.

THE HEIGHTS AND THE DEEPS

THIS is the summit, wild and lone.
Westward the Cumbrian mountains stand.
Let me look eastward on mine own
　　Ancestral land.

O sing me songs, O tell me tales,
Of yonder valleys at my feet!
She was a daughter of these dales,
　　A daughter sweet.

Oft did she speak of homesteads there,
And faces that her childhood knew.
She speaks no more; and scarce I dare
　　To deem it true,

That somehow she can still behold
Sunlight and moonlight, earth and sea,
Which were among the gifts untold
    She gave to me.

THE CAPTIVE'S DREAM

FROM birth we have his captives been :
For freedom, vain to strive !
This is our chamber : windows five
Look forth on his demesne ;
And each to its own several hue
Translates the outward scene.
We cannot once the landscape view
Save with the painted panes between.

Ah, if there be indeed
Beyond one darksome door a secret stair,
That, winding to the battlements, shall lead
Hence to pure light, free air !
This is the master hope, or the supreme despair.

TO MRS. HERBERT STUDD

AMID the billowing leagues of Sarum Plain
I read the heroic songs, which he, the bard *
Of your own house and lineage, lovingly
Hath fashioned, out of Ireland's deeds and dreams,
And her far glories, and her ancient tears.

  The sheep-bells tinkled in the fold.   Hard by,
A whimpering pewit's desultory wing
Made loneliness more manifestly lone.

  Friend, would you judge your poets, try them
       thus :
Read them where rolls the moorland, or the main !
Not light is then their ordeal, so to stand

* Mr. Aubrey de Vere.

275

TO MRS. HERBERT STUDD

Neighboured by these large natural Presences ;

Nor transitory their honour, who, like him,

No inch of spiritual stature lose,

Measured against the eternal amplitudes,

And tested by the clear and healthful sky.

THE UNKNOWN GOD

WHEN, overarched by gorgeous night,
  I wave my trivial self away;
When all I was to all men's sight
  Shares the erasure of the day;
Then do I cast my cumbering load,
Then do I gain a sense of God.

Not him that with fantastic boasts
  A sombre people dreamed they knew;
The mere barbaric God of Hosts
  That edged their sword and braced their thew:
A God they pitted 'gainst a swarm
Of neighbour Gods less vast of arm:

THE UNKNOWN GOD

A God like some imperious king,
  Wroth, were his realm not duly awed :
A God for ever hearkening
  Unto his self-commanded land ;
A God for ever jealous grown
Of carven wood and graven stone ;

A God whose ghost, in arch and aisle,
  Yet haunts his temple—and his tomb :
But follows in a little while
  Odin and Zeus to equal doom ;
A God of kindred seed and line :
Man's giant shadow, hailed divine.

O streaming worlds, O crowded sky,
  O Life, and mine own soul's abyss,
Myself am scarce so small that I
  Should bow to Deity like this !
This my Begetter ? This was what
Man in his violent youth begot.

THE UNKNOWN GOD

The God I know of, I shall ne'er
  Know, though he dwells exceeding nigh.
Raise thou the stone and find me there,
  Cleave thou the wood and there am I.
Yea, in my flesh his spirit doth flow,
Too near, too far, for me to know.

Whate'er my deeds, I am not sure
  That I can pleasure him or vex :
I that must use a speech so poor
  It narrows the Supreme with sex.
Notes he the good or ill in man ?
To hope he cares is all I can.

I hope—with fear.   For did I trust
  This vision granted me at birth,
The sire of heaven would seem less just
  Than many a faulty son of earth.
And so he seems indeed !   But then.
I trust it not, this bounded ken.

THE UNKNOWN GOD

And dreaming much, I never dare
  To dream that in my prisoned soul
The flutter of a trembling prayer
  Can move the Mind that is the Whole.
Though kneeling nations watch and yearn,
Does the primordial purpose turn?

Best by remembering God, say some,
  We keep our high imperial lot.
Fortune, I fear, hath oftenest come
  When we forgot—when we forgot!
A lovelier faith their happier crown,
But history laughs and weeps it down!

Know they not well, how seven times seven,
  Wronging our mighty arms with rust,
We dared not do the work of heaven
  Lest heaven should hurl us in the dust?
The work of heaven! 'Tis waiting still
The sanction of the heavenly will.

THE UNKNOWN GOD

Unmeet to be profaned by praise
  Is he whose coils the world enfold:
The God on whom I ever gaze,
  The God I never once behold:
Above the cloud, beneath the clod:
The Unknown God, the Unknown God.

TO THOMAS BAILEY ALDRICH

TO THOMAS BAILEY ALDRICH

IN ANSWER TO HIS SONNET "ON READING 'THE PURPLE EAST'"

IDLE the churlish leagues 'twixt you and me,
Singer most rich in charm, most rich in grace!
What though I cannot see you face to face?
Allow my boast, that one in blood are we!
One by that secret consanguinity
Which binds the children of melodious race,
And knows not the fortuities of place,
And cold interposition of the sea.
You are my noble kinsman in the lyre:
Forgive the kinsman's freedom that I use,
Adventuring these imperfect thanks, who late,
Singing a nation's woe, in wonder and ire,—
Against me half the wise and all the great,—
Sang not alone, for with me was your muse.

THE HOPE OF THE WORLD

I

HIGHER than heaven they sit,
  Life and her consort Law;
And One whose countenance lit
  In mine more perfect awe,
I fain had deemed their peer,
  Beside them throned above:
Ev'n him who casts out fear,
  Unconquerable Love.
Ah, 'twas on earth alone that I his beauty saw.

II

On earth, in homes of men,
  In hearts that crave and die.

THE HOPE OF THE WORLD

Dwells he not also, then,
  With Godhead, throned on high?
This and but this I know:
  His face I see not there:
Here find I him below,
  Nor find him otherwhere:
Born of an aching world, Pain's bridegroom,
  Death's ally.

III

Did Heaven vouchsafe some sign
  That through all Nature's frame
Boundless ascent benign
  Is everywhere her aim,
Such as man hopes it here,
  Where he from beasts hath risen,
Then might I read full clear,
  Ev'n in my sensual prison,
That Life and Law and Love are one symphonious
  name.

IV

Such sign hath Heaven yet lent?
  Nay, on this earth, are we
So sure 'tis real ascent
  And inmost gain we see?
'Gainst Evil striving still,
  Some spoils of war we wrest:
Not to discover Ill
  Were haply state as blest.
We vaunt, o'er doubtful foes, a dubious victory.

V

In cave and bosky dene
  Of old there crept and ran
The gibbering form obscene
  That was and was not man.
With fairer covering clad
  The desert beasts went by;

THE HOPE OF THE WORLD

The couchant lion had
　　More speculative eye,
And goodlier speech the birds, than we when we
　　began.

A flattering dream were this—
　　That Earth, from primal bloom,
With pangs of prescient bliss
　　Divined us in her womb;
That fostering powers have made
　　Our fate their secret care,
And wooed us, grade by grade,
　　Up winding stair on stair:
But not for golden fancies iron truths make room.

VII

Rather, some random throw
　　Of heedless Nature's die
'Twould seem, that from so low
　　Hath lifted man so high.

286

THE HOPE OF THE WORLD

Through untold aeons vast
 She let him lurk and cower:
'Twould seem he climbed at last
 In mere fortuitous hour,
Child of a thousand chances 'neath the indifferent sky.

VIII

A soul so long deferred
 In his blind brain be bore,
It might have slept unstirred
 Ten million noontides more.
Yea, round him Darkness might
 Till now her folds have drawn,
O'er that enormous night
 So casual came the dawn,
Such hues of hap and hazard Man's Emergence wore!

IX

If, then, our rise from gloom
 Hath this capricious air,
What ground is mine to assume
 An upward process *there*,

THE HOPE OF THE WORLD

In yonder worlds that shine
From alien tracts of sky?
Nor ground to assume is mine
Nor warrant to deny.
Equal, my source of hope, my reason for despair.

X

And though within me here
Hope lingers unsubdued,
'Tis because airiest cheer
Suffices for her food !
As some adventurous flower,
On savage crag-side grown,
Seems nourished hour by hour
From its wild self alone,
So lives inveterate Hope, on her own hardihood.

XI

She tells me, whispering low :
" Wherefore and whence thou wast,
Thou shalt behold and know
When the great bridge is crossed.

For not in mockery He
    Thy gift of wondering gave,
Nor bade thine answer be
    The blank stare of the grave.
Thou shalt behold and know ; and find again thy lost."

XII

With rapt eyes fixed afar,
    She tells me : "Throughout Space,
Godward each peopled star
    Runs with thy Earth a race.
Wouldst have the goal so nigh,
    The course so smooth a field,
That Triumph should thereby
    One half its glory yield?
And can Life's pyramid soar all apex and no base?"

XIII

She saith : "Old dragons lie
    In bowers of pleasance curled ;
And dost thou ask me why?
    It is a Wizard's world !

289   T

Enchanted princes these,
 Who yet their scales shall cast,
And through his sorceries
 Die into kings at last.
Ambushed in Winter's heart the rose of June is
 furled."

Such are the tales she tells:
 Who trusts, the happier he:
But nought of *virtue* dwells
 In that felicity!
I think the harder feat
 Were his who should *withstand*
A voice so passing sweet,
 And so profuse a hand.—
Hope, I forego the wealth thou fling'st abroad so
 free!

Carry thy largesse hence,
 Light Giver! Let me learn

To abjure the opulence
    I have done nought to earn;
And on this world no more
    To cast ignoble slight,
Counting it but the door
    Of other worlds more bright.
Here, where I fail or conquer, here is my concern:

XVI

Here, where perhaps alone
    I conquer or I fail.
Here, o'er the dark Deep blown,
    I ask no perfumed gale;
I ask the unpampering breath
    That fits me to endure
Chance, and victorious Death,
    Life, and my doom obscure,
Who know not whence I am sped, nor to what port
    I sail.

AFTER DEFEAT *

PRAY, what chorus this? At the tragedy's end,
    what chorus?
Surely bewails it the brave, the unhappily starred,
    the abandoned
Sole unto fate, by yonder invincible kin of the
    vanquished?
Surely salutes it the fallen, not mocks the pro-
    tagonist prostrate?

Hark. "Make merry. Ye dreamed that a monster
    sickened: behold him
Rise, new-fanged. Make merry. A hero troubled
    and shamed you.

* Written at the close of the Græco-Turkish War.

AFTER DEFEAT

Jousting in desperate lists, he is trodden of giants
    in armour.
Mighty is Night. Make merry. The Dawn for a
    season is frustrate."

Thus, after all these ages, a pæan, a loud jubilation,
Mounts, from peoples bemused, to a heaven refrain-
    ing its thunder.

TO THE LADY KATHARINE MANNERS

TO THE LADY KATHARINE MANNERS

(With a Volume of the Author's Poems)

ON lake and fell the loud rains beat,
 And August closes rough and rude.
'Twas Summer's whim, to counterfeit
 The wilder hours her hours prelude.

And soon—pathetic last device
 Of greatness dead and puissance flown!—
She passes to her couch with thrice
 The pomp of coming to her throne.

But while, by mountain and by mere,
 Summer and you are hovering yet,
A vagrant Muse entreats your ear:
 Forgive her; and not quite forget!

294

TO THE LADY KATHARINE MANNERS

I would that nobler songs than these
    Her hands might proffer to your hands.
I would their notes were as the sea's;
    I know their faults are as the sands.

At least she prompts no vulgar strain;
    At least are noble themes her choice;
Nor hath she oped her lips in vain,
    For you take pleasure in her voice.

And she hath known the mountain-spell;
    The sky-enchantment hath she known.
It was her vow that she would dwell
    With greatest things, or dwell alone.

And various though her mundane lot,
    She counts herself benignly starred,—
All her vicissitudes forgot
        In your regard.

WINDERMERE, *August* 1897.

JUBILEE NIGHT IN WESTMORLAND

THROUGH that majestic and sonorous day,
When London was one gaze on her own joy,
I walked where yet is silence undeflowered,
In the lone places of the fells and meres;
And afterward ascended, night being come,
To where, high on a salient coign of crag,
Fuel was heaped as on some altar old
Whose immemorial priests propitiated
With unrecorded rites forgotten gods.
Darkly along the ridge the village folk
Had gathered, waiting till the unborn fire
Should, from its durance in the mother pine,
Leap; and anon was given the signal: thrice
A mimic meteor hissed aloft, and fell
All jewels, while the wondering hound that couched

JUBILEE NIGHT IN WESTMORLAND

Beside me lifted up his head and bayed
At the strange portent, with a voice that called
Far echoes forth, out of the hollow vales.
Then the piled timber blazed against the clouds,
Roaring, and oft, a monstrous madcap, shook
Hilarious sides, and showered ephemeral gold.
And one by one the mountain peaks forswore
Their vowed impassiveness, the mountain peaks
Confessed emotion, and I saw these kings
Doing perfervid homage to a Queen.
Long watched I, and at last to the sweet dale
Went down, with thoughts of two great women,
    thoughts
Of two great women who have ruled this land ;
Of her that mirrored a fantastic age,
The imperious, vehement, abounding Spirit,
Mightily made, but gusty as those winds,
Her wild allies that broke the spell of Spain ;
And her who sways, how silently ! a world
Dwarfing the glorious Tudor's queenliest dreams ;
Who, to her well-nigh more than mortal task,
Hath brought the strength-in-sweetness that prevails,

JUBILEE NIGHT IN WESTMORLAND

The regal will that royally can yield:
Mistress of many peoples, heritress
Of many thrones, wardress of many seas;
But destined, more melodiously than thus,
To be hereafter and for ever hailed,
When our imperial legend shall have fired
The lips of sage and poet, and when these
Shall, to an undispersing audience, sound
No sceptred name so winningly august
As Thine, my Queen, Victoria the Beloved!

BACH, IN THE FUGUES AND PRELUDES

CONTENTEDLY with strictest strands confined,
Sports in the sun that oceanic mind :
To leap their bourn these waves did never long,
Or roll against the stars their rockbound song.

APOLOGIA

THUS much I know: what dues soe'er be
    mine,
Of fame or of oblivion, Time the just,
Punctiliously assessing, shall award.
This have I doubted never; this is sure.
But one meanwhile shall chide me,—one shall
    curl
Superior lips,—because my handiwork,
The issue of my solitary toil,
The harvest of my spirit, even these
My numbers, are not something, good or ill,
Other than I have ever striven, in years
Lit by a conscious and a patient aim,
With hopes and with despairs, to fashion them;
Or, it may be, because I have full oft

APOLOGIA

In singers' selves found me a theme of song,
Holding these also to be very part
Of Nature's greatness, and accounting not
Their descants least heroical of deeds;
Or, yet again, because I bring nought new,
Save as each noontide or each Spring is new,
Into an old and iterative world,
And can but proffer unto whoso will
A cool and nowise turbid cup, from wells
Our fathers digged; and have not thought it
  shame
To tread in nobler footprints than mine own,
And travel by the light of purer eyes.
Ev'n such offences am I charged withal,
Till, breaking silence, I am moved to cry,
What would ye, then, my masters? Is the
  Muse
Fall'n to a thing of Mode, that must each year
Supplant her derelict self of yester-year?
Or do the mighty voices of old days
At last so tedious grow, that one whose lips
Inherit some far echo of their tones—

APOLOGIA

How far, how faint, none better knows than he
Who hath been nourished on their utterance
   — can
But irk the ears of such as care no more
The accent of dead greatness to recall?
If, with an ape's ambition, I rehearse
Their gestures, trick me in their stolen robes,
The sorry mime of their nobility,
Dishonouring whom I vainly emulate,
The poor imposture soon shall shrink revealed
In the ill grace with which their gems bestar
An abject brow; but if I be indeed
Their true descendant, as the veriest hind
May yet be sprung of kings, their lineaments
Will out, the signature of ancestry
Leap unobscured, and somewhat of themselves
In me, their lowly scion, live once more.
With grateful, not vainglorious joy, I dreamed
It did so live; and ev'n such pride was mine
As is next neighbour to humility.
For he that claims high lineage yet may feel
How thinned in the transmission is become

APOLOGIA

The ancient blood he boasts; how slight he
  stands
In the great shade of his majestic sires.
But it was mine endeavour so to sing
As if these lofty ones a moment stooped
From their still spheres, and undisdainful graced
My note with audience, nor incurious heard
Whether, degenerate irredeemably,
The faltering minstrel shamed his starry kin.
And though I be to these but as a knoll
About the feet of the high mountains, scarce
Remarked at all save when a valley cloud
Holds the high mountains hidden, and the knoll
Against the cloud shows briefly eminent;
Yet ev'n as they, I too, with constant heart,
And with no light or careless ministry,
Have served what seemed the Voice; and un-
  profane,
Have dedicated to melodious ends
All of myself that least ignoble was.
For though of faulty and of erring walk,
I have not suffered aught in me of frail

APOLOGIA

To blur my song; I have not paid the world
The evil and the insolent courtesy
Of offering it my baseness for a gift.
And unto such as think all Art is cold,
All music unimpassioned, if it breathe
An ardour not of Eros' lips, and glow
With fire not caught from Aphrodite's breast,
Be it enough to say, that in Man's life
Is room for great emotions unbegot
Of dalliance and embracement, unbegot
Ev'n of the purer nuptials of the soul;
And one not pale of blood, to human touch
Not tardily responsive, yet may know
A deeper transport and a mightier thrill
Than comes of commerce with mortality,
When, rapt from all relation with his kind,
All temporal and immediate circumstance,
In silence, in the visionary mood
That, flashing light on the dark deep, perceives
Order beyond this coil and errancy,
Isled from the fretful hour he stands alone
And hears the eternal movement, and beholds

APOLOGIA

Above him and around and at his feet,
In million-billowed consentaneousness,
The flowing, flowing, flowing of the world.

Such moments, are they not the peaks of life?
Enough for me, if on these pages fall
The shadow of the summits, and an air
Not dim from human hearth-fires sometimes blow.

THE END

www.ingramcontent.com/pod-product-compliance
Lightning Source LLC
Chambersburg PA
CBHW060528030726
47498CB00004B/1117